The Curious Chronicles of Curious Tales

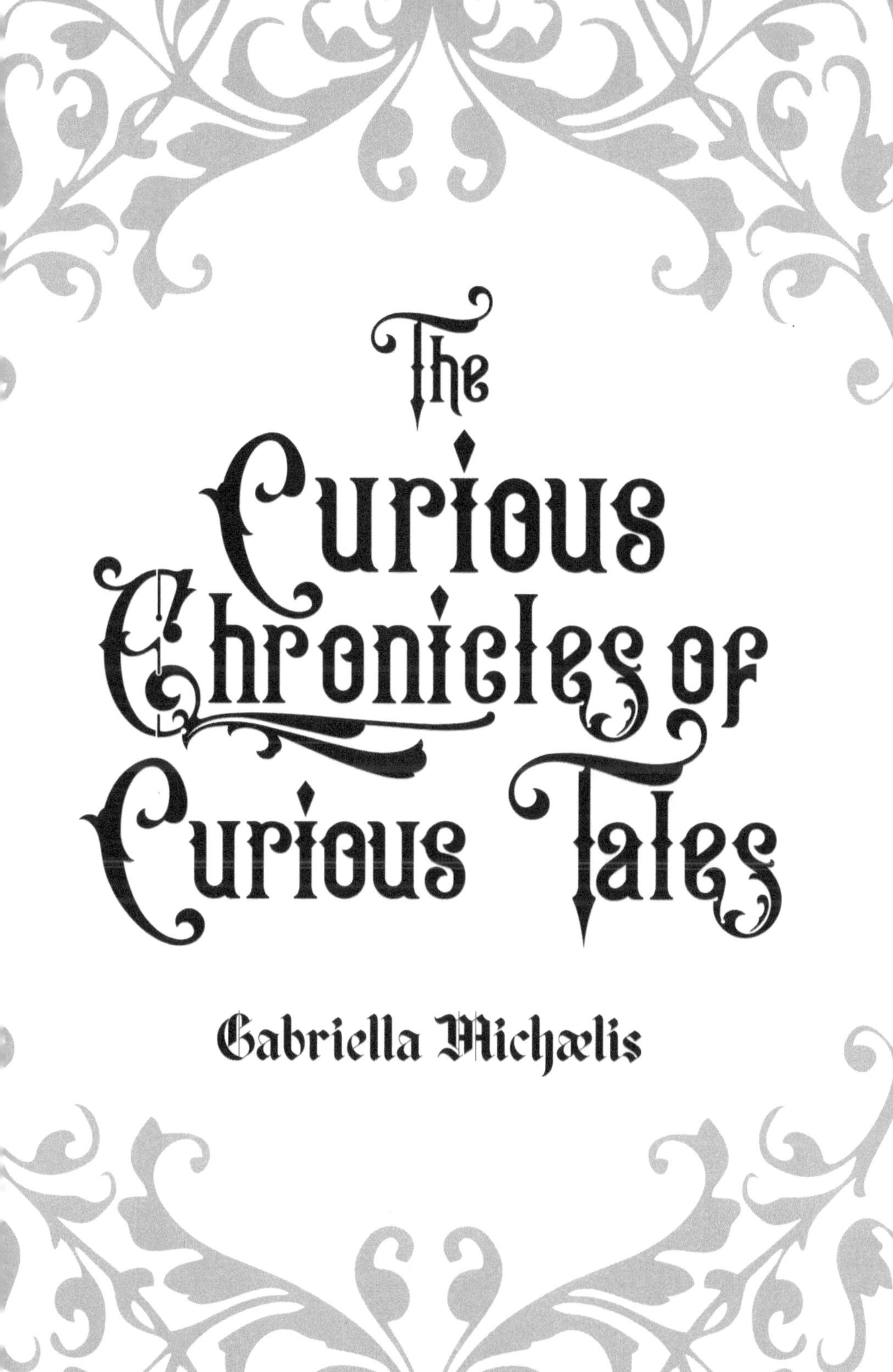

The Curious Chronicles of Curious Tales

Gabriella Michælis

*To all Wanderers and Wayfarers
who aren't afraid to dream, explore and believe.*

Introduction

How curious of you, Wayfarer, to have chosen this book to add to your collection.

This humble and most honored author can only imagine you were driven to do so by curiosity. This tells me three things about you:

1. You have no fear of the unknown (a necessary feat, should you wish to enter *my* world).

2. You are a lover of stories (which is most convenient, as I am as well).

3. You are always prepared to go on an adventure, and I truly hope you'll find one between these pages.

Beware though, to not let any of the hidden magic escape...

Have I caught your attention now, Wayfarer? I need you to hold on to your curiosity and sense of adventure, let your love for stories guide your way, as it did mine. Have an open heart and an open mind when you read the words I've woven, detailing my most unconventional journey to worlds beyond this one. My writings may not always be coherent, they may not always make sense, but, if you're a little mad like me, I trust you'll navigate your way through my sea of words with ease.

You may not believe the stories I have heard during my travels, but it is not your belief I need. It is your imagination I desire to spark in full force. It may not make much sense now, but your spark—the light that shines within all Wayfarers who navigate the Endless Stories of the Universe—might end up saving worlds.

Never lose your light.

Be fearless, for daring to take the first step into anything new might lead to greater adventures.

Always keep a look out when you walk in the woods, for you never know what kind of enchantments you may encounter.

And as is only logical to do in any traveling occasion, never be without a good book, or better yet, always be prepared to write one down.

Though the stories you will encounter here might be unusual, know that they are only a few grains of sand in a desert of greater stories yet to be told. To give birth to those stories would require that most treasured, most unique Spark of Imagination.

I sincerely hope your spark will turn into an almighty blaze, Wayfarer.

May these stories enchant you and open your eyes to discover worlds unseen before...

Cordially, and most humbly, yours,

– The Wanderlost Author

part one
Water

CHAPTER 1
the Journey

Once upon a time is far too archaic to start a story with these days, and yet, I suppose that makes it all the more enchanting to see at the beginning of a book. To understand my journey, 'Once upon a time' is exactly where we need to begin.

Once upon a time, there was a child who loved to play games with words. She put the letters together in strings, creating one word after another until they formed a chain of sentences and came to life as Stories.

If there was one consistent thing in my life, it would be that. Storytelling. Looking back now, there was never a time where I was without stories to tell, but I found myself always searching for a little more.

What else could a writer do but look out into the world in search of that special kind of inspiration, where stories were simply waiting to be written down?

Though my life has always been ordinary—and I have no delusions that that aspect would ever change—I found that the ordinary and the mundane dribbled into my writing. My stories, which I very much loved, lacked magic.

I wasn't a child anymore, and believing in magic and fantasy was considered uncomely by this modern world I found myself trying to fit into. Still, there was a part of me that believed in something more than meets the eye, that every fairytale in the existence of this world had some truth to them.

There was one time in my youth when I searched for a path that would lead me to something much greater. I thought I had seen someone then, walking through the forest, a little bewildered, a little lost. I don't know whether it was fantasy or just a faint memory. Not that it really matters.

I remembered the lessons I was taught by concerned parents, though I felt no danger coming from this stranger. Hooded in a cloak woven out of shadow and decorated with jewels made out of light, I was drawn to this mysterious figure. The jewels glittered and tinkled melodiously with each step like a gentle lullaby sung by a siren. I followed the hooded stranger, this enchanting pied piper, trying my best to keep up. But I blinked too often, and my young legs were too short to keep pace with the stranger's long strides. Thus, the cloaked person disappeared into the woods, taking the lullaby with them as the forest swallowed them whole.

Nevertheless, I felt something that day. A burst of exhilaration, a touch of fear, and the slightest but persistent sting of curiosity. Voices called for me, music playing unlike any I had ever heard before. It was little more than a whisper, and the words would haunt my memory forever: "The light in you is strong, but not strong enough yet to find the doors that lead to other worlds."

By the time I was deemed an 'adult' by society, I had long given up searching for worlds beyond the one we live in. I had to rely on my imagination to take me to these places I could only dream of traveling to.

Imagine my surprise then, if you will, when one day I found myself wandering through the very same woods where I had seen the stranger from my youth disappear like mist. I wasn't sure what brought me there, but it seemed that this time, the road beckoned me. The doors lay waiting, having been closed and denied to me before.

As any curious writer and lover of adventure would agree, I could not resist the call to find out if there was more to this world than we know. Perhaps taking a chance, a risk, could be worth something after all...

My journey to exploring new, fantastical worlds, started with a bluebird and a frog.

While I was making my way through that strange yet familiar forest, I came upon a small pond. The wind swept golden leaves from the forest floor, while others stuck to the damp earth. The smell of rain lingered in the air. There was nothing much impressive about the pond, save for the green frog that sat on a rock in the center, like a human would; legs crossed, arms crossed, as though it was leisurely enjoying a day out in the sun. While the sight was amusing, to say the very least, it became even more remarkable when I noticed a tiny, shiny, golden crown on top of the frog's head.

I stared at it, how its wide mouth formed a perpetual smile of relaxation. Its round, bulging eyes regarded me with a sense of tranquility I had never seen in a frog before. Fearing I might scare the princely frog away, I attempted to retreat from the odd spectacle. However, just as I put a good distance between myself and the frog, a small bluebird flitted before my face like a pixie, elegant with its stunning appearance. Its wings were a radiant, mesmerizing blue, the colors so bright, it appeared as though the bluebird had flown right out of a painting.

Unlike most birds, this one watched me with pretty, black eyes as it hovered inches from my face, head tilting from left to right. While this was uncommon, what struck me as most peculiar was the string of pearls around the bluebird's neck. It matched a delicate circlet, set with magnificent gems, upon the creature's head. At this point, I thought for certain I must be dreaming. If I was, I wasn't sure whether I wanted to wake up.

The bluebird flew towards the center of the pond, greeting the regal frog like an old friend. They bowed their heads to each other and the bluebird nuzzled the frog's cheek. Then, with its small talons, it lifted the amphibian off the rock. They looked at me before the bluebird turned and flew off, the frog croaking as if it told me to follow them.

Honestly, who was I to deny such a request?

What kind of writer would I be if I didn't follow a bluebird carrying a frog into the forest? Pages would remain empty forever if a writer didn't go on some adventures of their own, now and again.

Still in disbelief at what I was seeing, I grabbed the straps of my backpack. My feet automatically followed the strange pair deeper into the woods.

The bluebird was fast. It flew with such grace and strength, despite the extra weight. The regal frog still grinned, relaxing, as it let its friend do all the work.

The woods around me changed as I followed them. Colors faded like an old photograph and then brightened in technicolor all in a matter of seconds. The grass grew greener, the scent of pines grew stronger. The wind was gentler here, whispering songs of the forest as it brushed past me.

Perhaps I should have been frightened, walking deeper into a forest no longer familiar to me, but the child in me screamed to remember, screamed not to turn away and give up the search as I had so very long ago. Everything was so silent and peaceful around me, almost as if the world outside simply did not exist. Maybe, in that moment, it didn't.

I wish I could explain how it felt, standing in that enchanting, yet ominous clearing, surrounded by tall trees, while a bluebird and a frog turned to smile at me.

There were questions I wanted to ask, but I didn't know to whom I should direct them. For all I still knew, bluebirds and frogs lacked the communicative skills to speak to humans.

But I knew they wanted me to be here.

Perhaps they had seen me before when I was a child, roaming these woods while I was not yet allowed to go deeper to explore them.

Was my light strong enough this time?

I took a chance.

"Do you know what I'm looking for?" I asked.

The bluebird and the frog stared at me, saying nothing. Then, slowly, the bluebird descended, putting the frog down ever so gently on a tree stump, before landing beside him. The moment it did so, something bubbled from beneath the earth, startling me.

Around the base of the tree stump, water started to flow, creating a crystal clear pond. The bluebird chirped and the frog croaked, as water slithered upward like aquatic serpents, forming a tall arch over the pair.

Water filled the arch until it looked like a beautifully framed mirror, the glass flowing and rippling rings with the slightest touch of the wind. I saw cities reflected in the full-length glass, rain forests and purple mountains dusted in snow. I saw Earth in all its splendor, but something pulled at me from within the mirror portal, beckoning me to step closer, urging me to investigate the undiscovered worlds that lay waiting on the other side. My own curiosity betrayed me.

Or, did it save me?

The bluebird and the frog stood on either side of the portal, waiting patiently until I stepped forward.

I suppose there was always a point in one's life where fantasy and reality blur together, but this was pushing it. Even for me.

"I shouldn't..."

The hesitation came from the adult-side of me, the side that believed in rationality and reality. There was no room for fantasy, enchanting worlds, and stories. But, the writer-side? *That* side was dangerous. That side was pushing me forward, that side was laughing at the rational side, mocking it for its limited sense of imagination. The writer-side told me that everything I was seeing now was impossible, but, wasn't it great to see it anyway?

The bluebird and the frog bowed their heads when I approached the archway. I saw myself in the reflection of the water, the rippling of the glassy surface muddling my appearance, mixing the warm golden hue of my skin with the deep chocolate tones of my hair. In my dark eyes shone worlds unknown and stories untold. Then I did what every respectable writer would do. With a notebook and pen well-secured in my backpack, I stepped forward to begin my very own adventure...

CHAPTER 2
Wanderlost Borough

I thought I had woken up from a dream after passing through the mirror portal, as the environment had not changed as I hoped it would.

If I didn't know any better, I'd say the forest I stood in now was the same as the one from before. The only difference was that I could not find the archway, nor the bluebird, nor the frog anywhere.

Had I been imagining it after all? Surely, my mind would not have come up with something so vivid, only to rip it away from me again so brutally?

Looking around, and with nowhere else to go, I continued on my journey towards an unknown destination. I could only hope if I just kept walking forward, I'd stumble upon a road, or other people that could lead the way.

I paused.

Which way would that be, exactly? I had no idea where I was, so how could I possibly know which way to go?

This has to be a dream...

I pondered on what I just experienced and felt the frustration wash over me as if I was tumbling inside a massive maelstrom, unable to comprehend any of my thoughts. I couldn't make any sense of what I had seen.

The sky above me was a brilliant blue, though the sun shone gently like it was about to set on the horizon behind the crisscrossing of deep green trees. Did that make any sense? Or was I just searching for something to be different and magical so as not to feel embarrassed for having believed in a dream?

As my trek through the quiet forest drew on, I was ready to give up hope of finding something exciting. I guess I should have known that when the hero of a story hits a low point in their quest, a miracle appears.

Mine appeared on the horizon, twinkling softly like sequins in the sun, cozily snuggled in the valley at the foot of a magnificent mountain. My hope and excitement rekindled, giving energy to my tired legs. You see, the land I came from is a flat land, always battling against the unpredictable water of the seas that wish to reclaim its territory. There were no mountains there. That could only mean I had left my home behind and entered somewhere new.

I rushed toward the green hills. Unafraid and—most likely—unwise, I ran to the town that lay glittering like a beacon for wanderers who've lost their way.

Bulbs of light seemed to float over this old town, winking and dim. From afar, I would've mistaken them for stars. The hamlet appeared to have been built around an imposing bell tower reaching up to the sky as if it were a keep for imprisoned princesses. Green vines climbed up the old stones of the tower, their leaves interchanging in gold and red, covering an entire side of the edifice. At the top of the tower stood stone statues, overseeing each corner of the winds.

A medieval wall surrounded the town, vines and wild flowers

growing from the cracks and crevices. Upon closer inspection, the stone buildings and houses were decorated with half-timbered gables in various colors, some lined up in mesmerizing patterns. No house was the same. Wooden carvings decorated the roofs and pillars and even the cobbled streets shone like they were made of marble.

I felt my heart beat with excitement, though my mind was still in disbelief at my discovery. The town looked like it was transported straight out of a fairytale.

This time, I made sure to pinch myself, but even then, I was smiling.

I was utterly, irrevocably, out of my mind mad, but you are reading the words of a writer, a storyteller. You didn't truly expect someone woefully sane, did you?

It was my madness that appreciated the town I was roaming in. Though it made no sense to have found it so conveniently, I didn't rightly care what was logical, and what wasn't. I was far too distracted by the archaic buildings, the scent of fresh flowers and delicious baked goods in the air. My mind was focused on a want to explore. My feet suffered from that familiar itch to go traveling, my usual sense of wanderlust mercilessly taking over.

Where was I?

Where had the bluebird and the frog led me to?

Before you start accusing me of being hooked on some kind of hallucinogenic, know that I was under no influences when I found my way through the forest into this magical town. Keep in mind it is not your belief I seek as I share my experiences with you. I merely write down what I've seen, and can only hope you'll join me on the adventure.

There were lessons to be learned here. Stories to be found. I felt it in the air, I sensed it all around me.

The quaint old town seemed to be used to strangers visiting, with signs at nearly every corner, every wall, pointing in all possible directions you could imagine. I had never seen so many signs in one town before. Would they really lead to so many different destinations?

Now that I was actually walking through the abandoned streets, I noticed the charming buildings were actually rather rustic. Though, perhaps that was too generous a term. Paint was peeling off the walls, roof tiles were missing and gardens were left unattended. Some of the taller houses, squeezed together in a row to form narrow alleyways, leaned against each other as though they would crumble down, were they to stand alone. Still, amongst all of this, the scattered signs drew my attention the most. I was intrigued by them. I wanted to know why they were posted in multitudes.

Some of them looked new and polished, others gathered dust and thick cobwebs. Some signs were old and rotten, others taken over by the many vines slithering on the walls. There were signs with gilded letters, even more with just painted words. There were so many in fact, my mind was spinning with all the roads I could pick from. I read the signs carefully, to the best of my abilities, wondering how I could ever choose a journey to go on.

My happiness and excitement only dwindled for a second when I saw a sign that bore one word, gleaming in corroded metal: *HOME*.

Having been so utterly swept away by the magical things I had encountered, I had not stopped to realize I had no way of knowing how to go back home. It seemed silly to think about it, considering my desire to explore brought me to where I was now. However, wasn't the point of an adventure not only to have one, but to be able to return from one in satisfaction as well? How was I going to find my way home after this?

The archway made of mirrored glass had vanished after I passed through it, leaving me stranded. The thought dawned on me then that if I wanted to find the way home, I had to prepare myself for anything this confusing, but exciting path might throw at me. Daunting as that may be, I was more determined than ever to let all of this wash over me.

The first thing I had to do was to find out where I was before knowing where to go.

I let the signs guide me, following those that instinctively felt right until I arrived at an open square, wreaths of unlit light bulbs and colorful flags hanging over it, coming together over a corroded statue of winged people and mythical creatures. Small trinkets hung from these wreaths and it wasn't until I stood under them that I noticed they were gilded tools of writing: pens, pencils, quills, even pieces of shining coal, in various shapes and sizes.

Amongst the many signs that even decorated the pedestal of the imposing statue, my eye was caught by the biggest sign of them all. It was proudly displayed upon the roof of a Baroque-styled town hall, right under the enormous bell tower. The edifice appeared to be made out of a peculiar cream-colored stone, with sapphire-tiled roofs and decorated with golden ornaments which have seen better days. Despite all of this, the town hall still emanated an air of majesty.

The letters on the sign were beautifully etched and colored in gleaming gold, a stark contrast to its rather decrepit surroundings.

Welcome all Wanderers, great and small!
It's Wanderlost Borough to soften your fall.

"Wanderlost Borough?" I murmured, stepping back.
The bell started tolling. A wind swept through the town, like a

librarian blowing dust off of the most ancient of books.

In that moment, the town, which had lain dormant since my arrival, came to life. After the bell finished, people filed into the streets as if they were about to start the day. Perhaps this wasn't something I should have been so astonished about, save for the fact that the stars started twinkling in the azure sky; the moon gently shone with a smile on her face.

I stepped back again when the doors of the town hall opened widely and a cheerful man bounded through them. I couldn't help but smile at him—how his round belly jiggled when he moved, his grin appearing wider underneath the curly mustache that graced his upper lip. His friendly eyes twinkled when he caught sight of me. I froze, not knowing what to do, suddenly feeling very much like a trespasser.

"How lovely!" he exclaimed, approaching me, before dropping into a bow. "A new face, a new smile, an old friend!"

Too stunned to reply, I grinned at him like an idiot, barely managing to return the polite bow. I gasped when garlands of light were turned on as the night steadily approached. The light gave the gilded writing tools a soft, sparkling shine, their reflections shimmering on the ground and on the buildings around it. As if the town wasn't enchanting enough before, it simply glowed now.

"Do you like the light?" the cheerful man asked, hooking his thumbs underneath his suspenders.

"Oh, yes, it's quite beautiful," I replied, watching people walk the streets. They all wore smiles on their faces as they spoke to each other. Some even lugged heavy sacks or pushed large vending carts around. Were they heading to sell their wares on a market somewhere?

"We're very fond of the light here in Wanderlost Borough." The man flinched when one of the light bulbs above us wavered weakly.

He fidgeted with his suspenders and recovered the smile on his face, though there was something nervous about it this time.

"It seems that our light has drawn yours in," he said, taking a moment to appraise me. "You must be a seeker of adventure, dauntless and brave, for our guardians to have sent you here!"

I chuckled and shuffled my feet. "Actually, I'm just a writer. I suppose you could say I've wandered to your town, a little lost." I was surprised when the man blasted out a wholehearted laugh at my attempted joke, slapping his knee.

"A writer! Of course! I welcome you most warmly to Wanderlost Borough. You've come at a most wondrous time!" He loudly cleared his throat when the lights flickered around the town again.

"Does that happen often?" I asked.

He chuckled and dismissed it with a wave of his hand. "No need to worry about that, I assure you. I've been the mayor of this town for many decades and I fear that, since Wanderlost Borough has existed since the dawn of time, there's a little wear and tear here and there. So"—he wrung his hands—"you're a writer?"

I pretended to flow along with his sudden change of topic, but I noted the anxiety that shimmered in his warm eyes.

"Yes, I am. Though I'm not entirely sure how I got here, or *why* I got here, if that makes any sense." I said, as his mustache curled up even more when he beamed.

"Well, I reckon it's to write stories, as this is your profession, is it not?" He winked at me. "There are many journeys here for you to take, just pick a direction and go on your way."

"That easy, huh?" I was only a little skeptical. "Say I want to make sure I can go back home after this. Would simply choosing a direction work the same way to get there?"

"Ah..." His eyes sparkled in mirth. "You truly have no idea how lost you are, do you?"

I watched the man in silence, unsure how to respond. He started to laugh.

"Tell me, Writer, if you took all this trouble to find Wanderlost Borough, why are you now in such a hurry to go back home?" He hummed in amusement at seeing me so lost for words.

"Well, I had no idea I would find this town here," I said, fidgeting with my scarf. "And I will need to go back home, eventually."

"Yes, *eventually*. What a wonderful word that is," he said. "Wanderlost Borough is a town that was specially made for Wanderers like you, you know. You need not worry about how you will find your way back home. Experience often shows that those who are utterly lost, always manage to find their destinations. It just takes them a little longer."

"I see..." I watched him a moment. The mayor was so comfortable around me, though we were strangers to one another. "So, you're telling me that while I'm here anyway, I should just find a path to take and see where I'll end up?"

"That is what most Wanderers do, yes." He nodded, the both of us looking up at the lights as they palpitated now. It was as if they struggled to stay lit. The mayor told me not to worry about the light, but even the people walking around had stopped to look at the garlands above. When the ground shook lightly, the people started clamoring, their voices ringing with concern and panic. I kept my balance during the tremor, but it faded away as quickly as it arrived.

"I suppose you'll tell me not to worry about that, either?" I asked the mayor, who, despite being visibly shaken himself, attempted to mask his worry behind that smile. Looking up at the lights now, they appeared to have dimmed, casting deep shadows around the town. I squinted at them.

"Do the shadows tremble and dance in Wanderlost Borough?" I looked at the mayor for a second and followed his gaze to a pair of shadows moving about without a source to have caused the motion.

The shadows looked like two small entities, dancing on the cord that was cast by the wreaths above before they disappeared into the black.

"More vigorously than we would like," he remarked reluctantly. "You are most welcome in our humble town, young writer, but I must urge you to find a path. You will find many stories to write here, and I implore you to do so with a warm and open heart. As long as you do that, you will find your way back home, I promise you this." Something struck me as odd with his little speech. The cheerfulness in him had diminished, leaving behind an air of suspicion.

"Is there something wrong with this town, Mr. Mayor?"

"Oh, my child," he started, letting out a sad laugh as he straightened his clothing and brushed the dust from his shoulders. "Our story will be told once you've heard others first."

I wish I had asked him more when he looked at me that time. His mustache curled upward slightly. The man rocked back and forth with his toes and the heels of his feet. There was something sorrowful in his eyes, something he desperately tried to mask. He told me I had come to Wanderlost Borough at a most wondrous time. But something told me that may not be the case. I opened my mouth to speak again, when a small shadow suddenly drew my attention.

"Did you see that?" I asked.

He followed my gaze but shook his head, lifting his shoulders. "I see nothing, young writer."

"There! That shadow, it's moving! It's crawling!" I pointed, but the mayor would not even look.

With a straight face, he shrugged again. "There's nothing there.

Perhaps it was your imagination?" Something mysterious lingered in his gaze before he bowed and turned back toward the old town hall.

"Wait, you're leaving—huh?" I turned my head quickly when I saw the small shadow crawling over the cobblestones and diving up as if the ground was made out of water. It took a proper shape now and I gasped at the sight of a small, lizard-like dragon. Though it was colored black from head to toe, its bulging eyes were a bright yellow. Its tiny wings flapped erratically about as it hissed at me.

"What a strange creature..."

It approached me and looked up with its big, round eyes full of curiosity. I carefully reached out to the little dragon, curious to feel its scales, curious to see if it was real.

The creature closed its eyes and waited, allowing me to touch it. Then, it snapped at my fingers and crawled up my arm, quick as lightning. I attempted to shake the wretched creature off, but it fell down on its own. I thought I had been successful in chasing it away, until I saw my notebook in its mouth.

"What in the world? Hey! Come back here!" I ran after it. In spite of my haste to catch the draconic thief, I managed to read the sign pointing towards the direction I was pursuing the dragon: *WAY FAIRGROUNDS.*

CHAPTER 3
the Way Fairgrounds

"**S**top! Thief!"

Yelling like a maniac whilst running through the otherwise tranquil streets was probably not the right way to make friends with the locals, but what else was there for me to do? The nasty, thieving dragon fled so fast I needed to run with all my might to keep an eye on it.

I'm reluctant to admit it, but running is not my most favorite way to pass the time. In fact, I do not believe it is a way to pass time at all. I believe running is only to be done in case of danger or in case of having to pursue things, like wretched thieves who have stolen important notebooks.

Panting as I went, my lungs burning and legs aching—I'm a writer, not an athlete!—the pesky dragon led me to an open part of Wanderlost Borough.

I paused for a moment to catch my breath, only to have it taken away from me again when I gazed around my new environment. I was in the middle of a bustling market and fairground. The smell of caramel and chocolate overwhelmed my senses, and the sounds of chattering and music were so pleasant, it made me want to explore. I wanted to browse through the alluring carts that sold trinkets beyond my imagination and comprehension. I wanted to comb through the book stalls and stroke the pages of books I had never heard of before. I allowed my attention to be stolen away by a few eye-catching titles.

Beware When the Ogre Sleeps: An Anthology, The Whims of Pegasi Explained, "Once Upon Forever..." Collected Stories by Fairy Folk, Nox Codex: Myth of Soul Slayers.

The cart rolled away before I could reach out to the books, and I noticed there were stalls surrounding me, exhibiting odd contraptions, inventions that seemed too magical to be deemed fully technical. While I was busy gawking at the splendor around me, the screech of a little thief snapped me back into focus.

The dragon made off with my notebook, slipping through the crowds like a shadow. I made my way through the throngs of people, noticing how their brocade clothes lacked a certain shine. Despite the many colors they wore, none of them looked vivid. Uneasy mutterings flowed through the crowds when the lights sputtered overhead.

What was wrong with the town?

The dragon knocked over vases further ahead, the crash betraying its position. I tried not to shove the people out of the way, slipping past them to not lose sight of the creature. There were signposts here as well, but I was too flustered to read them all.

"Come back here!" I yelled at the hissing dragon, whom no one else seemed to notice. "I need that!"

As I ran after the beast, I slowly became aware that it led me away from the market and the fairground, away from the people and the sounds and scents of civilization. I stopped for a moment to catch my breath a second time, conveniently in front of another sign.

While I was on the brink of passing out, I noticed the dragon had turned around and stopped as well. Its head tilted to the side as if it wondered what was taking me so long.

"If you can wait for me, you can give me back what you stole, you little sneak thief!" My anger earned only another hiss as a reply.

I breathed out, trying to steady my pulse. I looked at the sign in front of me.

"'This way to the Way Fairgrounds'? I thought we just left that behind us?" I said. "That way to the Way Fairgrounds?" Another sign pointed to a different direction altogether. "What is this, Wonderland?"

The larcenous dragon shrieked loudly.

"Argh, you puny pest!" I gathered whatever strength I had left in me and chased it into the woods. I didn't know how a small creature like that had the capacity to keep ahead of me, but I knew as soon as it used its wings and flew away, I would never get my notebook back. It forced me to chase it up hills, going higher and higher, and damn it all to kingdom come, I was sure the thing was taunting me.

Every time I stopped in dire need for rest, it simply waited a few feet ahead of me, the notebook clutched between its fangs. It ran off again the moment it saw I had the energy to chase it once more. It wasn't until I found myself standing at the top of a massive cliff that I ceased the chase, with the world quite literally at my feet.

The misty, thick clouds rolled in front of me to mask the beautiful landscape below, like an ocean in its movement. It reminded me how high up I was. The view of the trees and hills engulfed in wispy nimbuses while the last light of the sun shone on them was breathtakingly spectacular. It was unfortunate that the sight of the black dragon ruined the mood. The beastie even had the audacity to sit down at the edge of the cliff to enjoy the view as well.

I snuck up on it as quietly as I could. I winced when its tail flinched and it turned to face me. When it hissed at me again, I snapped.

"There's nowhere for you to go, so hand over my notebook and I'll forget this ever happened!"

The dragon tilted its head and its yellow eyes inspected me. "For... get," it mimicked, the sound of its voice tiny and distorted. It cleared its throat, coughing and gurgling as it went. "For-get!" it repeated, like a toddler who had just learned a new favorite word. I, on the other hand, was less enthused and a lot more confused.

"You can...talk?" It was my turn to tilt my head in curiosity at the creature.

"Forget," it repeated quite flawlessly. "Forget, forget!"

"Great, a parrot dragon! That's cute." I exhaled deeply. "Now, give me back my notebook." I said it as gently as I could, approaching the creature slowly. The dragon closed its jaws a little tighter around the notebook, staring at me. It shook its wings and flared them open, as lead dropped in my stomach.

"Forget!" it spoke with a muffled voice before it swung its head and threw my notebook off the cliff.

"No!" Panic settled into every fiber of my being, my voice echoing in the massive silence. I stopped just at the edge of the chasm, absolutely stunned at the surprising sight before me. My notebook floated atop the clouds.

"That's not—that's not possible!" I stammered, watching the dragon lift off, flying toward the notebook and grabbing it again, with its talons this time. It sat easily down while the clouds rippled and rolled under its butt as though they were made of sturdy cotton balls.

"No way..." My blood froze in my veins, my body tingling in utter tension at the thought I had to take the first step onto these clouds to get my notebook back.

Was this really worth it all? It wasn't like I couldn't get another notebook to write in, right?

"Forget! Forget!" The dragon mocked me. I groaned and looked down at the rolling clouds, swirls of vapor reminding me how wispy they were. Could they be thick enough to be solid? It just didn't compute to me how water vapor and ice crystals could possibly hold my weight. If I stepped on them, I'd fall, and die. The physics were not hard to understand this way. The dragon could mock me all it wanted, but it had wings to keep it afloat. I, obviously, lacked that luxury.

The dragon waited with my notebook, watching me.

"I'm not going over there to follow you," I told it firmly.

The dragon waited calmly, head tilted ever so slightly.

"How are you even doing that?!" I grabbed a pebble and threw it. The pebble bounced off the wispy billows, but it didn't fall. Maybe I was too naive in thinking these were clouds. Maybe they were clouds, but covering a larger part of the cliff? Though I thought I had seen the valley below before it was shrouded, I could have easily been mistaken.

How else could the dragon sit on clouds? Why had my notebook not fallen down when the dragon threw it?

Why did you follow a frog and a bluebird through the woods? Why did you step through that mirror portal made out of water?

"Oh, this is madness," I said to myself, taking a shaky step forward. I grabbed the straps of my backpack, shuffling forward inch by inch. Using one foot I felt around the surface. Seeing the wisps disperse was not a convincing sign.

"Okay, just take one step. If that stupid dragon can do this, then you can, as well." I crushed my eyes shut, squealing pre-emptively the moment I set my foot down on the clouds.

Laughing like a nervous idiot, I looked beneath me. My foot was planted on puffy softness. "It worked!" I wiped the sweat off my brow, gathering myself. Feeling the sturdiness below my feet gave me the courage to walk unsteadily toward the dragon who still waited for me to catch up with it.

"I bet that was entertaining for you to watch, eh?" I shuffled forward, still afraid that any wrong movement might send me plummeting down.

The dragon chittered as I walked on the clouds to reach it, and for some reason, the annoying beast didn't flee when I approached. It simply allowed me to grab my notebook. I held it to my chest, glaring at the dragon while doing so.

"Forget?" it said, the pitch high at the end of the word as if it was asking me something.

"I'd like to forget you, yes," I said. I grumbled at being surrounded by a sea of billowy mist. I suppose it would be useless to remind myself I had a fear of heights. I already started to turn around when the dragon shrilled again, taking flight and hovering before me.

"Forget," it repeated, but how was I supposed to know what it was trying to say?

Frustrated and tired, I wanted to tell the pesky beast off, when I noticed something glimmering behind it. I hadn't seen the structure before since the clouds rolled and swirled like a thick fog around me. The sight started to clear, making it easier for me to peek behind a thin shroud of vapor. The dragon turned as if showing me what lay beyond the horizon was its intention all along.

From the clouds rose a magnificent tree, as pure as white pearls, with ivory leaves bearing golden veins. The bark appeared to be scaled with silver, and little orbs of light were attached between its branches. I found myself drawn to it. The dragon was following me, whispering the word "forget" now and again.

"Wow…" I smiled at such beauty and magnificence. I moved faster to reach the tree, my hand already outstretched. My smile faded as soon as it had come, when I saw that some of the orbs borne by the tree looked rotten and tainted by something filthy.

What happened to it?

I had barely thought the question before the comfortable, solid feeling underneath my feet started to crumble.

"Oh no…" I looked down in panic. As if the clouds had remembered they were never meant to be solid in the first place, they began to disperse and turned into thin veils of mists, which, as you may guess, did not bode well for me at all.

Running as fast as I could to get away from the tree, toward the safety of the ridge, I soon found myself running uselessly on air. My heart thumped in my chest and in my desperation I reached out to the flying dragon, who had the heart at least to clasp its talons around me.

But to no avail.

I heard it squawking at me as I fell, no wings to help me, no clouds to catch me.

I disappeared through the mist.

part two

Sky

CHAPTER 4

Storyteller

I died before I could decently start my epic adventure.

Well, at least I thought I had.

Give a traveling writer some slack, would you? It was my first time traveling to different worlds, after all. How was I supposed to know that tiny dragons could give someone so much grief?

How was I to know clouds weren't strong enough to support a human's weig—Okay, granted, I did know that, but how could I have known that same rule applied to other fantastical worlds as well?

Groaning, I slowly blinked my eyes open without knowing what to expect. The first thing I saw was the sky. While the sight was shielded by the canopy of leaves from mighty, tall trees, I could tell it was a clear day. Not a cloud in sight. The cliff had disappeared and there was no sign of the white tree either.

I carefully moved around until I was certain I felt no pain, then I sat up. My brown leather backpack sat neatly beside me. Even the bunny keychain seemed to have survived the fall.

Letting out a deep breath, I rubbed the back of my head, scanning my new environment. If I truly did die from that fall, I didn't imagine the afterlife would look like this. There was neither a gate nor a horde of angels to guide my way (or demons, sometimes I feel I could swing both ways). There was no bright light at the end of a tunnel either. Instead, softer, glimmering, twinkles of light floated through the air like fireflies. When I reached out to one of them, I noticed they weren't insects at all. Literal specks of light were just hovering about like living organisms.

"Huh, pretty..." I smiled when a small cluster of them gathered around my hand, feeling like soft feathers stroking my skin.

Maybe this was some kind of afterlife after all? Or, a limbo, of some sorts? I mean, how had I come out of that fall alive?

I grabbed my backpack before patting my clothes in search of my notebook. I was rummaging through my bag when something scratched and hissed nearby. I turned around to see the little black dragon, nibbling on something. Big yellow eyes blinked at me, the notebook hanging from the creature's mouth.

If I had truly died, then this truly was my hell. The muscle beneath my eye started to twitch. I grabbed a stick and charged at the dragon, crying out to scare it. Instead of just dropping the darned book, the dragon bit tighter into it, running away from me.

"Get back here and give me back my book, you lizard!" I yelled as it flew up the thick branch of a tree, the kind of which I had never seen before.

"Forget!" it squawked as I stomped my foot.

"Believe me, I'm trying!" I threw the branch at it and, of course, my aim was impeccably off, leaving me with little else to do but sulk. The dragon remained perched on the tree, snuggling against an impressive, glowing orb that grew between the trunk and branches.

Where am I now?

I sighed, staring up at the tree. It stood strong and tall, rooted firmly in the ground. Several orbs of light were perched in the tree, and though they were beautiful to look at, it made me wonder whether I was still in Wanderlost Borough. I hadn't seen massive trees like this one, with dark thick branches that coiled whichever way they desired. Long, willowy tresses fell from the tips of those branches like green waterfalls. The leaves shimmered as if coated by silver wax.

I touched the trunk of the tree, surprised at how warm it felt. I heard the dragon scrambling above me and I considered following. I had never gone through this much trouble in retrieving a notebook, but that thing meant the world to me. When I scribbled in that particular notebook, I always felt like the words were magic. Everything flowed out of my pen, inspiration spilling as easily as ink. Other notebooks didn't do that for me.

"All right, I'll play your game, you overgrown gecko!" I stretched and cracked my knuckles, grabbing the tree and lifting my foot.

"Hello."

Yelping, I stumbled back and fell over.

"Oh, forgive me, I had no intention of scaring you." A woman dressed in white giggled.

Where the heck did she come from?!

After the initial shock wore off, I recovered and got back to my feet while doing my best not to fumble around too much. "N-no, it's quite all right, you didn't scare me." My voice was shaking. I doubted whether she believed me—I knew I wouldn't. On top of that, my face was probably glowing bright red by now.

"So I see." The mysterious woman gave nothing away and only smiled. She raised an eyebrow when she looked up at the tree. A chuckle escaped her lips upon seeing the dragon, huddled around an orb, never parting with my notebook.

I took the moment to study her. She was clad entirely in a white cloak that covered the clothes she wore underneath. It fell over her shoulders like a blanket of freshly fallen snow, delicately embroidered by silver and golden brocades at the edges. Her hair was a pale silver with an icy shine to it, but what struck me most was her face. While kind and gentle, it seemed ever-changing somehow, like there was a veil over her face that could only be seen when it was focused on.

"Aha, I see my devious friend has been causing trouble again."

My eyes widened. I pointed at the dragon. "You know that thing? Is it your pet?"

"Oh, no, I wouldn't ever call him my pet, but we do have an amicable relationship. Most of the time." The woman reached out her hand and the small dragon regarded us with interest. "Come now, you know better than to take things that do not belong to you." Her voice was soothing, yet firm, when she reprimanded the dragon.

I glared at the little beast as it approached, its tail curled around my notebook. The dragon hissed characteristically at the woman, though it walked onto her outstretched hand anyway, crawling over her arm until it perched itself neatly on her shoulder.

The woman took my notebook from the dragon and shook her head at the beast. "I turn my back for one second and you disappear from my sight. Where have you been?"

The dragon grumbled defiantly, flapping its wings and throwing its face away.

"Don't pay him any mind, child," the woman said, finally handing over my notebook.

"I'll try my best not to," I replied, hugging the book against my chest. "Thank you. I thought he'd never let it go."

"Oh, this little one means no harm. He's just very playful, that's all." She glanced at the dragon when it bit her collar in protest. She patted the grumbling creature's head and turned back to me.

"I saw you fall from the sky," she said, "that must have been quite a journey."

I gaped at her before gazing up. "You saw me fall? How did I survive that?"

"With a tremendous amount of luck, I'd imagine." The woman chuckled, stroking the little dragon as she appraised me. "You're oddly dressed, if you don't mind me saying so. I've never seen clothing like yours before."

My cheeks heated, feeling self-conscious. My pink plaid scarf hung loose over my neck, the ends dragging over the forest floor. The hooded black jacket I wore was unzipped, but covered with dried leaves and dirt. A trickle of shame fluttered over me when I compared my everyday attire of jeans and a black shirt to the woman's snow white garments she seemed to have borrowed from a lady out of a fantasy story. I looked like a disheveled beggar next to her.

"Ah, yes, well..." Was I allowed to tell her I wasn't from this world? How would the rules work here?

What if she has never seen someone like me before? How am I going to explain? What if I already broke some fundamental laws of the universe here?

"Where are you from?" she asked. She didn't seem scared or worried at all. In fact, she breathed tranquility and grace, calming my own nerves. She sat down on top of a boulder near the great tree while she waited for my answer. Then she gestured for me to sit opposite her.

"Well, just recently I fell from the sky, I suppose," I started, rubbing my head. "Before that I was in a town called Wanderlost Borough. Then I chased your little friend to the Way Fairgrounds, and I suppose that's where I still am?"

The woman looked at me quizzically. "What strange names. You are most definitely not from this world."

Her announcement startled me, but she only laughed, pointing at me as if she had discovered something.

"I have heard tales of people like you," she said, while clusters of light moved toward her. I sat frozen, looking at actual magic unfold right in front of my eyes.

"Y-you have?" I asked.

She nodded, a mysterious smile on her lips. She moved the light, shaping it until the image of a white tree shone above the palm of her hand.

"Hey! I know that tree! I mean, I saw it before I fell." I looked at the woman, sinking down on the boulder across her. The moss was soft where I sat and I bit the bottom of my lip as I tried to figure out the trick of the light. "How are you doing this, with the light?" I was far too intrigued and curious to think of anything else now.

"The light is a friend of mine." The white tree rotated on her palm, a perfect miniature version of the one I saw before. I reached out to the image, touching it briefly. A gasp escaped from my lips when I could actually feel the tiny leaves and the smooth, silvery bark of the pearlescent tree. The woman watched me closely before she nodded.

"So, this is how it must be then," she said.

"Excuse me?"

She took a deep breath. "You are a Collector. Many Mythicas before me told tales of Wanderers who fell from the sky to collect stories, then move on to tell their tales to other Wayfarers. They do this to spread a little knowledge, a little light, and a lot of magic into various worlds. I am most honored by your presence here, as confusing as it may be to you."

With me gawking dumbly at the woman, I tried my utmost to

understand what she was saying. "That's a very fanciful way of describing a writer." I let out a nervous laugh. "Wait, what's a Mythica?"

At this, the woman straightened, while more floating lights gathered around her and she bowed her head.

"I am a Mythica," she said with a proud smile on her face, though the black dragon on her shoulder rolled its eyes and yawned, utterly unimpressed. "I am a Storyteller. I work with the light to paint pictures as I tell the stories."

"I see!" I nodded with enthusiasm. "So, in a way, you're a writer, too."

She shook her head. "No. Though we are similar, I cannot share my stories the same way you could, but I am glad to meet a kindred soul." She spoke while watching the floating lights approach me.

"What is this world? Where are we right now?" I was convinced now that Wanderlost Borough was far behind me.

"You are in a world where light and darkness exist in delicate balance with one another," she explained. The pearl tree still rotated gently in place.

Awakened by curiosity, fidgeting with the notebook in my hand, I scooted forward. Dozens of questions flooded my mind, as though a levee had broken.

"Light and darkness?"

"Yes. This world was born in light, a beacon of life and majesty." Her eyes shifted, staring at something in the distance only she could see. "That was until a darkness slithered its way over the world, tainting the light, feeding off the life that gave this world its shine."

My mind was ablaze with questions now, but before I could ask them all in rapid succession, I noticed something strange about the image of the white tree. While its color was still pristine, some of the leaves had turned pale and ashen, crumbling down.

Wondering whether it was the Mythica who had done this on purpose, I caught her desolate stare.

"Is that meant to happen?"

"No, it is not," she whispered, a rueful look on her face. "This tree is unique to our world, like the Willoak tree we're sitting under. However, the Istoria Arbor is one of its kind. It's a sacred tree, planted by the very first Mythica in existence."

I scooted forward even further now, unable to tear my eyes off the enchanting tree. "How did Mythicas come to be? Is this world filled with people like you?"

A sad smile appeared on the kind woman's face. "There are very few of us left, unfortunately. Though, I would love to tell you the story, if you really wish."

I nodded eagerly, fidgeting with the notebook as I bit my lip. She looked at my lap.

Her voice was urgent, and it pushed me to grab my pen, hovering it over the paper.

"Will you tell this story to others, Wanderer? Will you tell our stories, even after you've left?"

"I don't know who to tell the stories to, but I'll write them down, with your permission."

The woman placed her hand over mine, giving an enthusiastic nod. "Make sure to remember every word."

"Forget!" the dragon interjected, squawking in protest when the woman flicked its snout. Annoyed, the little creature left her shoulder and, instead, crawled over to mine. It nestled comfortably there, eyes already gazing at the blank pages.

"Are you ready, Wanderer?" the Mythica asked.

With my pen and notebook already prepared and a dragon on

my shoulder, I nodded, and thus I chronicled the first tale into my collection.

CHAPTER 5

the tale of the
First Mythica

Eventide is a country that always found itself battling against the darkness.

During the creation of the world, the light that brought life only had so much left to spare for this majestic nation in the far West. Although soft shimmering lights always glowed in the air, they were weak, fragile. Still, their shine was revered and respected.

Light kept the monsters at bay.

While the proud folk of Eventide were natural-born fighters with fire running through their veins, the monsters, roaming the shadows in those ancient times were creatures truly to be feared. Those swallowed by their darkness, never returned to the light.

In a country of twilight, where the sun never shone to its full potential, the fierce clans of Eventide battled each other for territories that basked in floating lights and Willoak trees, large shining orbs perched amongst their mighty branches. It was the belief that those who possessed the light were the strongest in the land. The monsters would not attack those settlements and the people would be safe for another day.

It was for this very reason that the small settlement of Cielune was always on its guard and always prepared to fight off intruders or vicious robbers. While there weren't a lot of floating lights there and Willoak trees were sparse, there was one thing Cielune possessed that other settlements did not. Strewn across the fertile lands of the settlement were extraordinary gems named kristars— crystals that shone as brightly as the stars did. The people of Cielune mined them from deep, muddy caverns, and in the deepest, darkest bodies of water. Kristars were even found within the mountains, where rivers of scorching hot fire flowed. Their light was strong and guarded against the demons crawling in the night.

Many coveted Cielune and its fertile grounds, which was why its inhabitants trained themselves into becoming the greatest, and strongest warriors of Eventide. There was no tolerance for the lazy, no room for the weak, and there was definitely no place for daydreamers there.

How Keiana had not been exiled from Cielune, she didn't rightly know. If there was one thing the warriors of Cielune loathed more than a daydreamer, it would be a storyteller.

A daydreamer could be forced to take their head out of the clouds, but a storyteller?

Horrendous!

No matter how hard you tugged at them, storytellers were stuck in their dreamlands, and proudly told other people about it, too. And no one had time for stories when there were battles to fight and kristars to find.

If Keiana had not been their best forager, her neighbors would not have tolerated her presence as they had so far. She knew this, since they avoided her whenever possible. It was somewhat of a lonely life for the young woman, but she didn't mind much. In fact, Keiana often found her moments of solitude the best moments of her day. When she was alone, she could gather as many kristars as she was able, and set them all in half a circle around her. Since no one ever seemed interested in the stories she told, the glowing rocks made the perfect audience as they couldn't complain.

Keiana was a soft-spoken woman, wise for her age, and rather despised physical combat, but she was by no means ignorant about the complicated, turbulent time she lived in. She often had to defend herself and her territory against invaders, and though she had been successful thus far, she never liked the conflict. No matter how hard she tried persuading others that fighting over the light would only feed into the darkness, no one would listen to her. They'd much rather reach for their weapons and start hacking away instead.

Heaving a deep sigh, Keiana placed her latest batch of kristars in front of her. The gems shone so beautifully she took a moment to appreciate them. She loved the gentle blue tones of the kristars she found in the lake, though she was equally impressed by the red and orange light of the kristars she found inside the mountain. They reminded her of a blaze of fire. The ones she found in the earth always glowed green, and putting all three together never failed to attract the soft lights that floated around. They made her feel safe and comforted to such an extent that she could understand why Cielune was attacked so frequently.

Her thoughts were briefly interrupted by the sight of the sun beginning to set on the blue horizon. Darkness would come soon.

"As if we don't have enough to worry about, with what lurks in the dark, we even have to worry for our own people trying to attack us and take Cielune out from under our noses," she complained in a whisper, closing her eyes for a moment when a gentle breeze passed her by.

"What story shall I tell today?" She thought back to the things she had dreamt the night before. She watched the kristars twinkle, and took a deep breath.

"I could tell you the stories of our Gods. Or about the day I nearly met a dreaded water serpent that toils around in the underwater lands of the ocean." She smiled. "Maybe I could tell you about the time I encountered a Willoak tree and the light it carried sang to me..."

Keiana startled when the kristars pulsated brightly. She had never seen them do that before.

"Do you like it when I mention the light?" she asked jokingly, knowing full well that kristars were not living entities and could not understand anything she said.

The young woman scrambled backwards when the kristars rang like small bells caught in the wind. Keiana watched them for a moment, tapping some of them with the tip of her boot. Had she imagined it, or did she hear voices coming from the stones?

"Can you understand what I'm saying?" she asked, feeling only a little foolish for speaking to a bunch of glowing rocks.

Relieved, but slightly disappointed at the lack of a response, she sat back down.

"An empty stomach could deceive the eyes," she mumbled to herself, repeating what an elder had once said to her. She would have been satisfied with the explanation, were it not that she wasn't hungry at all.

After another moment of inspecting the kristars and finding nothing out of the ordinary, Keiana settled herself in front of them once more.

Just as she was about to begin, an intrusion from the darkness behind stopped her. Though she was never afraid of the night, she was wise enough to be wary of anything lurking in its shadow.

"Why must I always be interrupted?" Keiana grabbed her weapon, a long staff with three kristars adorning the top of it. They were sharpened to strike someone fatally if necessary. However, Keiana never used the tip of her staff to claim a life. She felt wrong to taint the beautiful light with the sin of crimson blood.

The night had settled in quickly today, much faster than she expected. She searched the skies for the triple moons. The biggest one only shone in the first quarter, the second one waxing and faint against it. The third moon was nowhere to be spotted and Keiana didn't like how this diminished the light.

The kristars on her staff glowed brighter than the moons did, a contrast compared to the murkiness around her. She tucked a lock of dark hair behind her ear, her hazel eyes shimmering against the light of the stones.

As she looked into the blackness of the woods, the eyes of nocturnal animals flashed back. Those posed no threat to her, but if intruders prowled about and saw the amount of kristars she had gathered, she knew she had to take care of the problem. It was better to be safe than sorry. Especially since she knew there were other things to be truly worried about.

Keiana's heart beat faster when she scanned the forest, anxious for the monsters she could not immediately see. How many of them would be lurking in the shadows right now? They had claimed so many lives in the past, destroyed the light for no other reason but to shed blood.

Perhaps she should head back home. There was a foul stench in the breeze that made her shiver, the woods too silent for her liking. Grabbing the kristars and putting them in her sack, Keiana used their shine to light her way.

There was something strange going on here. The night had come much too fast. She couldn't help but shiver as she crept through the woods.

The leaves rustled above her, branches creaking as the wind swept by. Fallen twigs snapped under the weight of scurrying woodland critters. The darkness was dense around her. The kristars shone brighter now, and while Keiana appreciated their luminescence, it brought something worrying to her attention.

"Where did the floating lights go?" Her whisper cut through the silence. Only the dim glow of the moons above her faintly illuminated the earth, the stars dotted delicately against a velvet backdrop. It unsettled her to see the world so dark and gloomy. The shimmering lights had always been a form of comfort, always managed to keep the darkness at bay. She had never seen the land without it and fear tightened in her chest.

What's going on here?

Perhaps it was her enthusiastic, storytelling imagination that caused her to move toward the darkness. Keiana thought she smelled another story to tell, but she feared it wasn't one she wanted to remember. Not having seen a single floating light since she entered the forest, her angst grew. Since she often walked the blurred line between reality and fantasy, she made sure to search for the lights before coming to the chilling conclusion that they were simply gone.

How was this even possible?

Ever since the creation of the world, Eventide was the country of floating lights. They had always existed and could not be doused, not even blown away to other nations. So, how could they have vanished?

Keiana continued creeping through the woods, desperately hoping to find a cluster of floating lights somewhere, but the further she ran into the forest, the darker her surroundings became. When she stopped to catch her breath, a cold sweat covered her body. In the pitch black, she was the only one still giving off light. The trees were thick here, their branches tall and heavy with great canopies of enormous leaves blocking out most of the stars and the moons.

Were it not for the kristars, Keiana might as well have been blind. Yet, at the same time, the lights drew so much attention to her, she might as well have been a beacon to those with malicious intents.

What could she do?

Not being able to douse the kristars, the only thing Keiana could think of was to head back to more familiar grounds, out of the darkness. If she was quick about it she could still get away before anyone could spot her.

"Just retrace your steps, Keiana." Holding out her staff to find the way, her grip tightened when a gruesome sound echoed through the darkness. Ahead of her, something slurped and gurgled beyond the trees. Sweat gathered at the back of her neck as she attempted to cover the kristars with her cloak.

The noises grew louder and feeling vulnerable and exposed, Keiana dropped to the ground, hiding behind a tree.

She should have gone home after she foraged the kristars. If she hadn't indulged in her ridiculous pastime of telling stories to a bunch of luminescent rocks, she wouldn't have been in this position. To make matters worse, it seemed like the kristars shone even brighter now—or had it grown darker?

She took slow, deep breaths to calm her nerves, before startling when the loud noises were accompanied by heavy footsteps.

As she looked around the inky darkness, the kristars on her staff suddenly doused. Stunned, Keiana removed the cloak, a lump in her throat when she touched the extinguished stones. Every fiber in her being screamed that danger was nearby—she had to go back to safety, to Cielune, but without any source of light she didn't know which way to go.

Keiana shook her staff in frustration, wishing she could see something, anything! She froze when a gust of wind followed the slurping noises, the familiar twinkle of floating lights dragged along by its force.

The lights!

Without skipping a beat, Keiana grabbed her chance and ran after it.

The smile of relief on her face soon faded when she saw it was not the wind blowing at the floating lights. She watched in terror as they disappeared into a gaping blackness before her, snuffed out like candles.

The warnings of the evil roaming in the deepest of shadows were no exaggeration. Keiana remembered all the stories, and even told some of them to others as well, but to see an actual demon prowling about her land, so close to her, wasn't as exhilarating as the stories made it out to be.

Terrified, she watched the light disappear into a formless shadow, little more than a stone's throw away. With the little sense she had left, Keiana dove behind some bushes. She could only hope the beast had not seen her.

The creature grunted and heaved, breathing deeply, absorbing all the air around it. In the dappled moonlight, its big claws flashed, four red eyes peering evilly about. It snarled and a vertical mouth opened, glimmering dust vanishing into the creature's jaws. Rows of teeth circled towards the inner part of the monster's mouth while it sucked in the air, stealing the floating lights, drowning everything into the dark.

Keiana couldn't believe her own eyes. She had never heard of a light-stealing monster before. The creatures of the dark were always frightened of anything they deemed too bright for their tastes, and yet here stood a ferocious beast, making a meal out of their treasured lights.

Would she stand a chance if she fought it? She was swift and armed, but the monster was large, and undoubtedly strong.

I can't just stand idly by!

While Keiana talked some courage into herself, something in the forest changed. The air grew heavy, like a massive weight threatening to crush her. Whatever had arrived in the forest just now, was immeasurably worse than the light-stealing monster.

Keiana observed this new malice as its silhouette glided forward, the woods deathly still. She took note of how tall it was, and how crooked its sharp, twisted horns were. The lackluster glow of the moonlight cast eerie shadows over the entity's face, giving off the illusion its horns were growing and coiling.

How many more monsters would she encounter in the dark?

The darkness was overbearing, and so very cold. Even if she did try to run, she wouldn't get far—unable to see, unable to get her bearing.

Would anyone at the settlement notice she was missing?

"Keep going, my pet." The icy voice of the stranger carried through the air. "Consume this dreadful radiance, remember the promise of our Sire."

The creature grunted at the voice, its vertical mouth widening further until its face was nearly split in half.

Keiana remained breathless, keeping as quiet as possible. She had never looked beyond the borders of Eventide, never worried about whatever foes might linger there. To hear this demon speak made her realize that she should have. With all the quarreling between the people of Eventide, no one ever once worried about threats from beyond the borders.

What 'Sire' did it speak of? Whom did this creature serve?

She shook her head and took another deep breath. This demon was planning something malicious, and with the mention of a 'Sire', Keiana guessed this concerned all of Eventide, not just Cielune. After all, if the light disappeared here, then darkness would rule. If darkness ruled, there would be no Eventide left. Whatever the case, time was of the essence and Keiana needed to tell the elders what she had witnessed without delay.

Gathering herself, she stole forward, hoping the monsters were distracted enough not to notice her inching away. She carefully turned around in the dark, but winced when her foot broke a few dry branches on the forest floor. She stopped cold in her tracks, shaking in her boots when the beastly pair looked in her direction. The weak lights cast deep shadows over their forms. They did not move, and Keiana prayed she had escaped their attention somehow. Quietly attempting to make a run for it, she gasped when a terrifying face showed itself, inches away from her.

She stumbled back, crawling away from the demon. Yellow eyes glistened at her from an arachnid face, while twisted, crooked horns throbbed softly as the creature inspected her.

"How delicious...a human." The horrid face drew nearer. Spiny protrusions on its jaw clacked against each other like clattering teeth.

"Back, demon!" Keiana said, holding out her staff as the gruesome shadow dragged a jagged talon over the kristars on top of it. With their shine lost, they looked like nothing more than mere stones.

"How blissful was your ignorance?" Its voice was but a whisper, chilling and frightening. Swirls of black mist oozed from the demon's facial protrusions. It crushed a floating light within its wiry fist. "How dull..."

Keiana's heart thundered in her chest. She swung her staff with a yell but the creature grasped it before the blow struck. The demon hadn't even looked up. Instead, it tightened its grip on the weapon, using it to pull her closer.

"I can feel your resolution waning with your precious light. You *perishables* reek of fear, growing weaker as your light dies."

Keiana struggled to get loose, wincing at the demon's foul breath. She had smelled blood and decay before, but never so intense, never so close.

"Tell me," it continued, "how does it feel to fear death? Does it creep like spiders over your skin? Does it suffocate you like a blanket of ghostly shadows?" The protrusions clicked together in rapid succession. Keiana grimaced. The beast was excited.

"Can you sense it? The feeling of dread as my Master grows stronger?"

"Who is your Master?" she dared ask. "Whom do you serve?"

The demon bared its teeth in what could only be an attempt to smile. The sight was so horrifying Keiana desperately tried to wriggle her staff free.

"Struggling is futile. The light can't protect you anymore." The demon's yellow eyes glowed even brighter, as if the darkness of the night was feeding it with power.

"Who is your Master?" Keiana asked again, a shudder shooting through her body. Shadows and black mist moved around her, growing darker and more dense.

The light was dying. The ashen kristars on her staff were proof of that.

You should have run away when you had the chance, Keiana...

"Running won't save you," the demon said, as if it could read her mind. "Let go of that light." The whispered words sounded tempting, like the seductive promises of a lover. Had Keiana not been staring at a terrifying creature transforming before her eyes, she might have conceded.

"Let me show you the world of my Master, a resurrection of a world drenched in darkness!" The shadows thickened and coiled.

The sickening energy sucked her breath away, choking her. In spite of struggling against the demon, her consciousness was slipping. Further and further she faded as the demon fed on her life force, on her very own light.

This was not the ending she ever imagined for herself. This was not how she thought she would die—alone, surrounded by nothing but darkness. No one deserved that. There had to be something she could do, find a way to escape— a way to breathe...

Keiana...

Your light is stronger than you know...

She whimpered for a breath of fresh air.

You are a teller of stories, creator of worlds. Do not let Destruction stand in your way.

Keiana, we have always listened to you. Now, listen to us.

Blinking, Keiana squinted at the kristars on her staff.

Were they glowing again? These voices, were they...? It couldn't be...!

Listen to us, Keiana. You are the First.

The First? Were her illusions the result of her body slowly shutting down? Why did death feel so...strange?

"No," she said, her voice strained and barely audible. "I must warn..."

"Give up the light, release it, walk away from it. Perish with it." The demon of shadows growled, tightening his grip. Black mist swirled around her, eating away at her life force.

Do not give in, Keiana. Children of Eventide fight in the deepest of darkness so the light will shine once more.

There!

The kristars on her staff pulsed with light like a brief heartbeat.

Were the kristars actually speaking to her?

"We fight...in the dark"—she gasped for breath, wrestling against the demon's grasp—"so the light will shine...again." Finding strength in those words, she pushed back against the stunned creature.

"You measly mealworm! You dare defy me?" Fuming, its eyes gleamed at her. "Your light does not protect you anymore. Shadows roam these lands now!"

Keiana grunted as she fought back, empowered by a newfound energy. She was inexplicably aware of the earth beneath her, the trees around her, as if Eventide itself had suddenly risen to embrace her. She sensed the lights trapped within the kristars. She heard their call and she felt their presence.

The monster felt the shift in energy as well, clattering its spine-like protrusions wildly against each other.

"Impossible! Your light should have died by now!" Its whispering voice bellowed into a loud roar, shaking her to her core. But when the darkness grew, a fire was set ablaze in Keiana's soul.

With a loud yell matching that of the creature, that fire spread to the kristars in the sack, and on her staff. The rocks shone so brightly, so intensely, they burst from their crystalized forms, soaring through the darkness like falling stars.

"What is this? Stop! Can you not see the beauty of the shadows? Let the darkness in, surrender to its forces!"

She glared at the horrid creature, her hand outstretched as she envisioned the lights burning brighter. "Not today."

The light soared toward the screeching demon as it turned to flee. Its thieving pet was left behind, but before it could follow its master's footsteps, Keiana turned her attention to it. She watched the light soar through the air and with a single thought of her mind, saw it transform into the shape of a mighty serpent. Made out of the brightest light Keiana had ever seen, the serpent slithered forward, opened its mouth and swallowed the monster whole, burning it to a crisp.

Clusters of floating lights returned, swirling around Keiana. She watched how over a dozen of strong burning lights hovered over the palm of her hand, forming into a glowing sphere, waiting for her command.

The kristars on her staff still remained, but those in her sack had disappeared. Watching the orb in her hand, she assumed that was what the rest of the rocks had become.

Panting, and unsure what had happened, Keiana gawked at the light, relief washing over her. She could have died if the light hadn't saved her.

During the attack, an old memory flooded her mind, a story she had often told about almost meeting a water serpent. She could see the body of the creature coiling and dancing in the water in her mind's eye. She remembered how its scales had glittered in the lake as the last rays of the sun shone upon it. When she faced the monsters, the light had turned into the very serpent from her memory. But how? Why?

Keiana moved her hand, squealing in shock when the light

followed her movement. Even more peculiar, she sensed the light as though they were living entities, as if they breathed, like the energy of the woods around her.

By some strange miracle, Keiana felt connected with her environment, the way they spoke softly to her, embracing her like she was part of the land. She grabbed her head.

"What just happened?" She leaned heavily against her staff as the new, floating lights drew closer to the orb in her hand. They burned brighter than they ever had before.

Do not fear us, Keiana.

The multitude of tiny, celestial voices nearly made her heart jump out of her chest. She clung to her staff as she looked at the lights, uncertain how to respond.

We are the remnants of the sparks that gave life to this world. We have waited so long for someone like you to arrive. Your coming was long foretold to us, the First who was worthy to listen to our voices, whose voice held stories waiting to be told.

"I don't understand," Keiana said. "What are you talking about? Why can I hear you?"

You chased away a foul shadow demon, a spawn from the most terrifying entity known in this world. You managed to fend it off with naught but light and your imagination. It was your belief that helped you.

Keiana looked at her hands. It was official; she had lost her mind. She sunk to her knees when the tiny voices started speaking again.

Why do you doubt? You, who chooses to tell stories filled with hope and wisdom, during a time when most of your kin prefer to pick up a sword?

There is no time for hesitation, Keiana. You are a Mythica, a Storyteller, a creator of worlds. You are one with this land and were chosen to spread the light while darkness attempts to swallow all life!

You must warn your people of the impending threat. The shadows are restless. They will not give in. Warn them, before it's too late.

"This is truly happening, isn't it?" Keiana asked the light, well aware of the shimmering dust circling around her. "Why did you choose me?"

Her heart filled with dread as she realized what a heavy burden was placed on her shoulders. Her people had always been a magicless folk, and yet here she was, speaking to the very things the world revered, wielding the powers of the light with just her imagination.

You were chosen because you know stories hold power.

"Stories?" She was shunned by her neighbors for her love of stories! How could they give her power?

The serpent came to life, did it not?

Keiana startled at the answer to the question she hadn't spoken out loud.

Warn your people, Keiana. Show them the strength of the First Mythica of Eventide. Hurry!

As the voices waned away, the shimmering lights formed a path before her, leading her back to her settlement. Keiana looked at the kristars on her staff, how they shone vigorously. She gripped the weapon tighter and didn't waste any more time. She rushed to the elders to tell them what had happened.

"I speak truthfully before this Council. Demons in the darkness are planning to steal Eventide's light and plunge it into the shadows!" Keiana stood before a band of older, solemn warriors, all of whom regarded her with exasperation.

"I see," one of them said, rubbing his bald head with a cloth. "And how is it exactly you fended off this fearsome shadow beast, hm?"

Keiana huffed, trying to remain as calm and as patient as possible. "I told you, Beorim, the light saved me!"

"The light you claimed another monster had been slurping up and had disappeared?" His response dripped with skepticism.

"Yes—Well, no, not exactly. The light of the kristars flickered back on, I don't know how, but it happened! The light listens to me, or rather, I can listen to it, and we help each other." She struggled over her own words, unsure how to properly explain the situation.

Beorim grunted. "The light listens to you." He looked at his fellow elders.

"Keiana, do you realize what you are telling us, child?" Another elder interjected. His look was not one of scorn, but of genuine concern.

"I know how ridiculous this sounds, Gorun, really, I do, but I'm not making this up!"

"Your useless fantasy ramblings have gone far enough, Keiana," Beorim interrupted, standing up. "If you want to be useful, stand guard around Cielune. Fight off the band of thugs and robbers that wish to take our land away from us."

Keiana's blood boiled. "Thieves will be the last thing on our minds if that demon and its lackeys continue to steal the light!"

"Keiana, enough," Gorun said, attempting to soothe her.

She shook her head. "I'm not lying! We're not the only ones in danger, the whole of Eventide—"

"—will perish and you're the grand hero of the story to save the day!" Beorim mocked. "Get your head out of the clouds, lass! We've no use for your fantasies here! If you hadn't a knack for retrieving kristars the way you do, you would've been left in the woods to fend for yourself!" he said, as Keiana held in her own anger to prevent from lashing out at the stubborn elder.

"I suggest you live in the real world now, away from your dreamland, and stop telling us your lies! If we want a bedtime story, we'll call for you. Otherwise, you'll do well to keep to yourself and to stay out of trouble!" Beorim pointed at her.

"But I—"

"I told you to keep quiet!"

"There's no need to yell at the girl, Beorim," Gorun said calmly. "I'm sure Keiana meant no harm. Her imagination ran away with her, that's all."

"But it didn't," Keiana persisted. "I'm not making this up, this isn't a story, this is real! Why won't you listen to me?"

"By the Gods, lass, one more word out of you and I'll—" Beorim raised his fist, but before he could finish his sentence, another warrior came running, interrupting the conversation.

"Elders, forgive the intrusion, but there is something you must see!"

The pale and terrified expression on the warrior's face told Keiana more than words could. The elders swiftly followed the warrior as she chased after them. They arrived at the valley, not far from the settlement, where they kept the gathered kristars safe. Their sacred light had gone out, the floating lights unable to escape a similar fate.

"Impossible! What happened?" Beorim grabbed a kristar, its shine completely gone.

"We heard strange sounds coming from the forest, but when we went to investigate and came back, the kristars had all just...died." The guard shrugged, a frown on his face.

Gorun looked at Keiana then, and the young woman jutted out her chin. She didn't need to tell him she was right after all, the regret of not having believed her was plain on his face.

"Those floating lights have all gone as well. What are we supposed to do now?" one of the warriors asked.

"The sound you heard in the woods," Keiana interjected over the panicked murmur of the crowd, "did it sound like Beorim trying to devour the soup and the bowl along with it?" She elicited a few snickers from the crowd as Beorim scoffed.

"As a matter of fact, yes! As if someone was trying to gulp down an entire lake," the guard said with a nod.

Keiana looked at the elders. "If we don't do something now, that fantasy story you wouldn't believe, will come true."

"The kristars on your staff have not dulled. Why?" Gorun noticed the stones shining brightly as he touched them.

"The light speaks to me. I wasn't lying, Gorun." Keiana's voice was soft. She felt a little strange saying those words out loud.

A grim look appeared on Beorim's face and as he opened his mouth to speak, he was interrupted again.

"Beorim!" A young girl ran towards the elders this time, panting as she went.

"What is it, small one?" Gorun asked.

The girl gasped for breath, her cheeks flushed. She held up a torch, the flames casting shadows on her tired face.

Finally, she pointed behind her. "Tamoh and his kin are marching toward us!"

"Tamoh? I thought we had settled our dispute with that band of brigands." Gorun looked to Beorim. "They should have gone home by now."

The man rubbed the back of his bald head. "We shouldn't have trusted those marauders. You give them a finger and they yearn for your arm!"

"They're encircling the settlement." Another guard arrived, sweat dripping from his brow. "We're being surrounded."

"All right, you lot, you know what that means. Up to arms! Defend Cielune with your life if you must!" The warriors prepared themselves at Beorim's words. They prepared for a battle that, Keiana knew, would be a waste of life and time.

Eventide's proud warriors had always been fractured, clans believing themselves the better fighter over the other. The people of Cielune were no different in this regard. They always thought themselves more powerful since they owned the lands where the kristars were mined. This never stopped other clans of Eventide trying to overrun them anyway, stealing the light if they could.

But this time, Keiana knew why they had come. Whether they had struck a bargain with the elders or managed to steal some of the kristars didn't matter. What use were they if they had stopped shining?

Warriors were roused from their slumber with the threat in the air, and the night grew ever dimmer. The sun wouldn't rise for a few more hours— the darkest hour was yet to come.

"If those scum think they can overpower us now that we are at our weakest, they have another thing coming!" Beorim bellowed.

Keiana shook her head. "No, wait! We shouldn't fight each other! We must band together to defeat the true enemy lingering in the dark!"

But she shouted in vain. No one bothered to listen to her.

Why would other clans march to their territory to start a fight now, of all times? Had that demon stolen the light in other parts of the country, too?

Where else would others go if their own light sources had

vanished?

An uneasy feeling slithered and coiled in her stomach. The answer to that question was painfully clear. "What am I supposed to do now?" Keiana whispered to the stones.

"Enemy approaching!"

"Already?" Keiana startled when she saw the orange glow of torches through the darkness of the forest. Men and women with war paint on their faces marched to meet them. They must be the band of brigands Beorim and Gorun mentioned earlier. An imposing man, twice Keiana's size, stepped forward from their line of defense. She could only guess he was their leader, barrel chested and tall as he was. He held up a large knapsack, eyes directed at the elders.

"You deceiving, pox-marked flap dragons! You think to outwit us with your treacherous lies? Do the lives of innocents mean nothing to you?" The leader stood tall as he bellowed at the elders. Keiana heard the tremor of rage in his voice.

"This coming from a doghearted hedge-pig like you?" Beorim roared back. "You ingrates dare to march to battle against us after we so mercifully granted your request?!"

"Merciful?!" The invading leader spat. "We came to you in good faith! We told you we need the light of the kristars to protect our people from the dark and the monsters lingering in it!"

"Aye! That's exactly what we gave you!"

The leader scoffed. "Shall I show you what you gave us?"

Keiana didn't like the threat laced within the leader's words when he reached into the knapsack. He hurled a large block of stone at Beorim, and for a moment Keiana was impressed at the reach of the throw. The rock clattered against Beorim's raised shield, the elder aghast at the sight of the doused kristar.

"If it is a fight you desire, Beorim, the Blunt Bludgeoner of Cielune, allow Tamoh, the Morning Star of Bronwynn, to fulfill that wish!" Tamoh flung the entire sack with another impressive throw at the elders before he bellowed a battle cry, his warriors standing at attention.

"Wait!" Keiana called out in despair. "This was not our fault! The light is dying! We shouldn't fight each other!" She was ignored as her kin prepared for battle.

Helpless to stop the hot-blooded tempers of the warriors, her own instinct kicked in when the first warriors charged forward.

The world slowed around her. For a moment, Keiana was an outsider, watching warriors clash their weapons against each other in the murky moonlight, shouting and attacking with deadly intent. The wind picked up from the East, the air so foul it raised goosebumps on her skin. The light of the orange torches were extinguished and all Keiana saw when she looked at the woods, was darkness. Deep, thick, suffocating darkness.

Malicious eyes glowed in the deep, staring back at her. The distinct clicking of spiny protrusions snapping at each other made her skin crawl. A pair of yellow beads flashed by. She jolted at the sound of malevolent laughter booming from the shadows.

This has to stop! A fight like this, the bloodshed—It's exactly what the darkness wants...

Gripping her staff tightly, Keiana moved to search for the elders as the rest of the world caught up to her. "Beorim! Gorun!" Avoiding the rain of arrows with trained agility, her eyes scanned for the elders. She made use of the glowing kristars on her weapon to navigate through the battlefield until she was blindsided from behind.

Her head rang as she was pinned down by a heavy weight. "Release me!" she grunted, feeling the hot breath of her attacker near her neck.

"Pretty lights from those stones, little one," a deep voice whispered in her ear. "Why don't you hand that over and I'll get out of your hair?"

Keiana never loosened the grip on her staff. She slammed her head back, biting through the pain of having hit her assailant's face and scrambled away from him.

"This is a mistake, there's no reason why we should fight over this." Keiana tried reasoning with her attacker, standing straight and holding her staff at the ready. He was a tall man, with skin the color of dark ale. He pointed a scimitar at her, but his eyes were fixed on the kristars.

"Do you know what crawls in the shadows, little one? The lights have been snuffed out! We came to Cielune for those kristars and you gave us dead stones!"

"We didn't! I know what lies in the darkness, I've seen it!" Keiana moved when he did as they waited for the other to strike. She noted the thoughtful look on his face, how he was the first person who actually seemed to be listening to her.

"It's coming," she said, making the words count. "Your people must have seen it too; the floating lights disappearing, the night growing darker, and now the kristars dousing—"

"Then you know we need the light just as much as you do! We will take it by force if we have to. You are not the only people in Eventide who need to protect themselves from the darkness!" The man raised his scimitar, and struck it down, but Keiana deflected the attack with her staff.

"Will you listen to me?!" She dodged another attack, the man grunting as he charged.

Twirling her staff, Keiana knocked him back, the kristars sparking when they clashed with the metal of his blade. The light shone stronger as Keiana's anger grew.

The man was a good fighter, and quick for his size. He lunged fearlessly forward, slashing his scimitar as he went. Keiana parried his attacks and dealt a blow against his head with the blunt edge of her staff.

The man wobbled unsteadily on his feet and she spun, planting a kick against his chest that knocked him flat on his back. An arrow whizzed past her, scraping the side of her cheek before it hit the base of a tree with a thud.

Keiana was swept away by the battle around her, the cries of warriors filling the air, the scraping of metal singing. Above all of that, she heard the creatures in the darkness, approaching, laughing, growing stronger as the night grew darker. Around her the fighting never ceased, men and women shedding blood needlessly while the real threat loomed over them.

"Enough!" She held her staff with both hands, the kristars glowing brightly under her command. She ignored the painful groan of her assailant, who squinted his eyes against the sudden flash. Light burst with the intensity of the midday sun, a flare so brilliant it lit up the area, rendering the raging battle to a standstill.

Warriors cried out at the blaze, squinting their eyes at the spectacle.

Keiana concentrated as she thought about what she had experienced, the images of her story reflecting off of the light. She had meant to show this to the elders, had Beorim not been so quick to dismiss her.

The warriors gawked at the projections, gasping in unison when she revealed the face of the frightening, light-stealing monster. Murmurs of disgust swept the field as she showed them the demon of the shadows next, and what he had told her. The light returned to the kristars of her staff, leaving Keiana out of breath.

"How did you do that?" her attacker asked, his eyes wide with shock. In the bright afterglow of the kristars, Keiana saw they were violet of color.

"I am Keiana of the settlement of Cielune. I am the First Mythica of these lands, a wielder of the light against the darkness. I am a storyteller." She licked her lips, straightening before she addressed the stunned warriors around her. "This is what I've been meaning to show you!" Her voice trembled, but she made sure to speak loudly, directing her gaze at Beorim and Gorun when she spotted them in the crowd.

"If we do not unite to fight our common enemy, those wretched scum crawling in the black of the forest will plunge this country into the abyss and make slaves of us all!"

"Nepherox," someone called out. "Captain of Cadavers, the Shadow Dweller—that's the creature you've shown us!"

A panicked murmur swept through the crowd. A tremor shot through Keiana's fingers, her staff growing heavy. Of course she had heard of the stories of the fearsome Nepherox, the demon in the night that fed off the light of men and women. She would never have assumed to survive an encounter with it.

He fears you.

The light soothed her frayed nerves and she regained her composure. "To serve their Master, Nepherox and his legion of demons have stolen the lights, crushed their brilliance. If we do not stop them we might as well kill each other. At least that death would be more merciful."

She read the fear on the faces around her, but when she looked at Gorun, he was smiling and bowed his head.

"With the lights gone, I have no doubt the monsters are already lurking in our woods." He directed himself to Tamoh, the barrel-chested leader, who approached him. "We must show them that warriors of Eventide do not fear the dark," he said. Voices of assent rang through the crowd.

"And how will we do this?" The large leader asked, gesturing around him. "There is no light. Even the fires fail. How can we get back the light they stole?"

"She seems to know the answer to everything, this Keiana of Cielune, the First Mythica."

Keiana glared at her attacker, who rubbed his chest where she had hit him. There was a cocky grin on his face when he looked back at her. She should have hit him harder.

"Go on, then. How do we get the light back?"

She was aware of the eyes on her, and while she felt the pressure rising, the soothing glow of the kristars on her staff brought her courage. They reminded her that she was chosen for this. The moment she doubted herself would be the moment she doomed her people.

"I-I'll find a way," she stammered, though she had stopped trembling.

"You'll have to do so quickly, lass," Beorim cut in. He pointed at the dark forest. "Trouble has arrived."

Barely had he uttered the words, when the forest came to life. Shadows moved, the trees bended. Growls and hisses cluttered the air as hundreds of gleaming eyes watched the warriors. Without any form of light, they were defenseless, the monsters free to roam. And to kill.

"I can't believe I have to cooperate with the likes of you," Beorim grumbled, glancing sideways at Tamoh.

"I would happily embed my morning star in your skull any other day, you old stink goat."

"I'd like to see you do that without a head, you toad-sucking fairy!"

"I guess we'll have to practice on those vermin first, eh?"

Beorim grunted. "Aye. We'll kill each other tomorrow."

The two men nodded at each other before barking orders at their warriors, preparing them for battle.

The monsters appeared from the cover of the woods. There were so many of them. Despicable demons in all shapes and gruesome sizes reared their heads at the warriors, growling and snarling.

What was in the darkness to have created such terrible creatures?

Keiana jumped with fright when a pair of hands grabbed her shoulders, turning her away from the forest.

"Gorun, what are you doing?"

"If what you said is really true, we depend on you to bring back the stolen light. The only thing we can do is provide a distraction long enough until you can find a way to make all the kristars shine once again," the elder said. "We're counting on you."

A rush of panic flowed through her veins. "I don't know, Gorun. I only know what the light told me. They never told me how to get it back."

"You'll find a way, Keiana. I have faith in you." He led her away from the battlefield. "You've always spoken to the light ever since you were a child. Your parents never knew what to make of it, and neither did I. But now I see." He held her hand and firmly squeezed it around her weapon. "I know you'll find a way. You're the most imaginative of us all, after all."

"Gorun..." Keiana started to speak, but the elder shook his head.

"Hurry, now! The valley contains the most kristars—start there."

She bit her lip and nodded, jumping lightly when her former attacker stood waiting beside her. "If you wish to fight again, I suggest you fight those monsters." She eyed him warily.

"I am Amani," he said, as though in way of apology. "I overheard your conversation. I have faith in my kinsmen to hold off those beasts while you find a way to wake up the light. I'll help you. You'll need a guardian." Realizing she needed all the help she could get, Keiana nodded and bowed to him.

"Come, Amani, we don't have much time." They ran towards the valley, a pair of yellow eyes following them from the shadows.

The valley of Cielune was a rich ground where kristars were gathered and grew freely. No matter how dark the night became, the valley always shone with a multitude of colored lights, brightening the sky. To see it so dull and dim was absolutely disheartening.

"How exactly are you planning to bring the light back to the land?" Amani asked.

"When I confronted Nepherox the first time, the light of the kristars burst to help me. The stones were gone, but the light stayed. I suppose I have to try to release the light lying dormant in the gemstones." Keiana took a deep breath. At the moment, that was the only plan she could think of. She only hoped it would work.

"And how do you release the light when there is no light left?" Amani asked again, the cynicism evident in his deep voice.

"I use my imagination, Amani. That seemed to work the first time I tried it." Keiana felt the pressure building up in her shoulders. If she had no way of releasing the lights, Eventide and its people would be lost forever.

Perhaps it was unfair for the light to put so much responsibility on the very first Mythica in existence, but it was to be expected that great power was always coupled with greater responsibility. The hero never had time to think or ponder about their actions. They needed to be quick and act accordingly to survive. Keiana was painfully aware of this.

"Tell stories," Keiana muttered to herself, "do what you do best..." She heard movements in the woods around them.

True to his word, Amani stood guard nearby, though Keiana wouldn't have blamed him if he had run away.

"Have you figured something out yet, Storyteller?" he asked. Gleaming eyes watched them from the shadows, growing larger and larger as they approached.

"I'm trying my best!"

"Try harder!"

Keiana scoffed in frustration.

"I don't know what to do," she whispered. "How can I bring back the light by telling stories? How can stories help with anything—" Keiana abruptly shut her mouth when a tiny kristar glimmered near her feet.

Could the answer be that simple? Would the light react if she told a story?

It shouldn't be any kind of story, she decided, planting her staff on the ground beside her. Her imagination caught fire, the words floating toward her, spinning a familiar tale.

"The light had died, and darkness crept over the land, attacking all that stood in its way," she started, a small smile playing on her lips when two kristars twinkled in response.

"Though the land was plunged into shadows, the people of Eventide would not give up without a fight. They put their trust in a foolish, stubborn storyteller, whom the light had chosen for reasons beyond her comprehension." She swallowed. Monsters snarled and growled from the woods behind her.

Amani kept his eyes on them, unsheathing another scimitar as he prepared for a fight. Keiana noted the beads of sweat glistening on his skin.

"What are you doing? Are you telling stories to those stones?" Amani regarded her, an eyebrow raised. "Have you lost your mind?!" He yelped when the first monsters jumped out of the woods to attack, but quickly regained his focus. Keiana tightened the grip on her staff, but she had to concentrate on the kristars.

Flustered, with panic threatening to overwhelm her, she watched Amani fend off the beasts, his scimitars dancing like they were alive. He slew the demons, one at a time before the assault suddenly stopped and the creatures retreated. While Amani caught his breath, Keiana felt this was no time to feel relieved. The shadows in the forest all started to grow and move, appearing to melt together, looming over them.

Focus, Keiana.

"S-s-stories—" She forced the words out of her mouth. "Come on, Keiana, you do this every day. You know how to tell a story, so do it!"

"Are you talking to yourself?!" Amani gawked at her in disbelief.

"I think I know how to save Eventide, do you mind?" Keiana yelled. Her eyes widened when another monster slithered through the shadow. "Amani!"

The man drove his two scimitars into the head of the horrid beast, and flung it away with a grunt. It disintegrated when it touched the kristars.

"We don't have much time left, little one! I can't fend off these beasts forever, you know!"

Keiana's own frustration boiled over, bringing her mind to focus.

"Realizing the storyteller had the ability to awaken and strengthen the light that was stolen—provided she wasn't consistently interrupted by a cheeky guard named Amani"—she glared at him for good measure, starting to feel the flow of the story glide out of her mouth—"the Mythica knew her storytelling came to good use, as there was a way to bring the light back."

Trusting in Amani to stand guard, Keiana concentrated on the kristars around her, seeing images in her mind glisten to life right in front of her. "With the help of the dormant kristars, the Mythica could create a tree of stories, unstoppable, indestructible, that would create shimmering lights as long as stories were told by a Mythica to others of this world." She imagined the tree with all her might. She envisioned the enormous trunk shooting upward, the roots coiling and gliding deep in the ground and over the valley. She pictured the branches dancing to the sky as delicate leaves decorated them. The kristars began shining again as the earth trembled.

The young woman laughed triumphantly. "It's working!"

Amani had gutted one monster, ready to attack another when the creature shrunk before his feet and crawled back into the darkness of the woods. Keiana smiled when he turned around, eyes wide with astonishment.

The valley twinkled like newly awoken stars, shining more radiant as the enormous tree grew taller. Its bark glinted like white pearls, climbing higher and higher with a rumble. The barren branches soon hung heavy with ivory leaves, golden veins pulsating through them.

"By the Gods..." Keiana heard Amani exclaim as she gazed happily at her creation. "The crazy lass has done it!"

"The crazy lass can hear you, you know," Keiana said, still standing a short distance away from him, surrounded by sparkling kristars.

A smile graced his full lips before his eyes widened in alarm.

"Keiana, watch out! Behind you!"

She turned, but the demon grabbed her collar, flinging her away. Nepherox hissed, slithering over the kristars. A black sludge was left in its wake.

"I gave you a choice, filth." The threat resonated through its raspy, gritty voice. The demon grew in size as it absorbed the lingering monsters hiding in the shadows. Spiky protrusions grew out of its spine and bended to the side like the legs of spiders.

"I told you to abandon the light. It cannot be brought back!"

"Why are there kristars glowing underneath you, then?" Keiana retaliated, crawling back to reach her fallen staff.

The demon brought down one of its legs to crush the stones underneath it. "You have done nothing. Your light will never be strong enough to defeat the darkness my Sire brings!"

Keiana reached her staff when the demon rushed forward and pierced her hand with one of its protrusions. She shrieked, her blood dripping over the kristars.

"Keiana!" Amani ran with his blades lifted to strike the demon from behind. Without even so much as glancing at the warrior, Nepherox waved its hand and Amani flew backwards. Monsters appeared from the black sludge trailing after Nepherox, and attacked him.

"What to do with such...weakness?" Nepherox's eyes gleamed as they gazed over Keiana's form. She struggled to get her hand loose, but the demon pressed further down. She cried out in pain.

Nepherox loomed over her, a despicable creature born of darkness. How could she have thought she was strong enough to defeat such malice?

Shadows danced before her vision, the glow of yellow eyes shining mockingly at her. The tree she had created wavered as the blackness glided toward it.

"You should have let the darkness drown you when you had the chance." Nepherox growled, pinning her further down.

Keiana...

She winced at the sound of the celestial voices. *I can't do this...*

"Let the light fade." Nepherox inhaled deeply and her throat tightened. Once more he fed on her life force. Her light.

Fight, Keiana! Finish your story!

The world blurred around her, hot tears spilling from her eyes. She strained herself, using whatever bit of strength she had left to struggle against the demon's grasp. She couldn't move.

Keiana...

"Keiana!" Amani's voice pierced through the haze of her mind. "Keep going!" His violet eyes shone with a fury. The kristars near his feet buzzed with energy. Even as he struggled against the monsters from the shadows, he looked strong and unrelenting. "The crazy Mythica created a white, sacred tree, born from the radiance of kristars, to forever shed light on Eventide once more..." He nodded encouragingly.

Nodding back, she turned to face Nepherox. The kristars pulsed around her. The tree rumbled as it shot up to the sky again.

"Who are you to defy the night?" Nepherox said. "Relinquish your life, abandon your hope!"

"I am Keiana," she said softly, focusing on the hum of light around her. "I am a Mythica, a Storyteller that creates entire worlds from thin air." She winced, the pain in her hands pulsing through her body. "I will create such a powerful beacon that will give birth to floating lights and make it stronger than ever before!"

Keiana yelled when she kicked the demon away, crying out in pain when its protrusion left her hand. As she scrambled to grab her staff, the kristars shone fiercely. Nepherox shrieked.

"Behold the birth of Istoria Arbor!" Her voice carried through the air, kristars bursting with light one after the other as the tree coiled to the heavens. "Each story told by a Mythica will create a new leaf, spreading more light across the land," she said. Lights burst in multitudes around her, ridding Amani of the monsters that assaulted him, causing Nepherox to shrink in fear. The demon snarled at her, but Keiana pushed through.

Ignoring the pain and sweat glistening on her brow, she marched toward Nepherox. The kristars on her staff sparked. The creature slipped miserably on its own muck, melting at the touch of the light.

The black ooze bubbled and spat when Nepherox moved. "Curse you!"

"Give in to the light," she said fiercely, shooting its wretched words back at the demon. "Darkness will not lay a finger on this land!" Keiana shot forward, her staff raised to strike.

Nepherox screeched and fled, dissolving into a black mass that slithered toward the Istoria Arbor.

"Get back here!" Keiana ran after it, but to no avail.

Nepherox laughed and fused itself to the tree, seeping through the roots. She watched helplessly as the tree was no longer hers alone, tarnished by the darkness.

"No!"

The golden veins transformed into black tendrils, Eventide's last hope of light waning before her eyes no matter what she did to try and strengthen it. She envisioned purging the tree from the darkness, but it wouldn't be cast out. She touched the trunk with her staff and even when the kristars sparked brightly, the demon remained within the tree.

"What happened?" Amani shouted, panting next to her.

"The Istoria Arbor! My creation—that coward fled into it and now it's eating away at it from the inside." Desperation slithered into Keiana's stomach. "I can't control it anymore."

Was this it? Had she failed everyone?

"There has to be a way to stop it poisoning the tree." Amani watched her.

Dulled by pain and fatigue, Keiana stared at her creation, her mind racing as the light pulsed erratically around her.

"Balance," she muttered unintelligibly, racking her brain.

"Balance?" Amani asked. Shaking his head, he grabbed Keiana by the shoulders. "How do we stop it?"

Keiana opened her mouth to answer, but her attention went to her staff. She leaned it toward Amani, frowning when the kristars pulsated.

He followed her movement before shaking her again. "Keiana, what do we do? If Nepherox manages to poison that tree, all of this has been for naught!"

"Poison," she repeated. "Of course! Amani, that's it!" Keiana ran toward the tree, sensing the incredible amount of energy radiating from it. She knew the answer now, she knew what had to be done to ensure the light could never fade again.

"What is it? What are you up to?" Amani caught up to her and grabbed her arm to pull her back.

"To counter poison, you need medicine," she answered, feeling a tranquil calm wash over her. The voices of the light spoke to her and she savored the sound. "Trust me, Amani. I know what to do. This is the way."

Keiana shivered, but for the first time in her life, she felt like she had finally found her place in the world.

Confused, Amani gazed at her. "I don't understand. What are

you—?" His eyes widened. "You can't! Think about what you're doing, Keiana. You might never come back again! Where will the people of Eventide be without someone like you?"

She managed a smile. "I don't think I'll have to return. Once the light has come back, the tree will make sure it can't ever disappear again." She took one more look at her staff before handing it over to Amani. "As for our people... I don't think there's any need for worry either."

At a loss for words, Amani took the weapon but still shook his head. "Is there no other way? What if this won't work?"

"It will work." Keiana smiled. "All I ask of you, is to tell my story. Can you do that?"

Amani hesitated before he tightened the grip on the staff and nodded. His violet eyes shone with determination.

Satisfied, Keiana took a deep breath and stepped toward the tree until she could nearly touch it. It hurt her to see her creation being defiled by the shadows of the demon. She saw Nepherox's face through the bark, but she wasn't frightened.

"Are you prepared to face the void, Storyteller? Will you join me in the nothingness?" Laughter echoed from the tree. Nepherox's face appeared and disappeared in waves. "My Master is already in this world. Oblivion comes..." The tree shuddered and creaked as if it were about to snap in two.

Keiana remained calm, feeling flecks of light shower over her like golden raindrops. "Oblivion may try, but you and your kind will steal the light of this land no more. Even when the rest of this world is drowning in shadows, this land and its people will remain strong. They will always fight, with the flames inside their hearts that you can never douse. They will fight for the light and will strengthen it, always." A jolt of determination coursed through her body when she uttered the promise. She smiled at the contorted face within the tree.

"You think you are a match for me?" Nepherox gurgled. The roots blackened further, but Keiana feared nothing. She felt the warmth and strength of the kristars at her feet, glowing radiantly in her presence.

"I know I am," she said, putting her hand on the bark as the roots coiled around her. The remaining kristars exploded into blinding lights. The wind swept up, tugging at her clothes, her dark hair flying up. The tree continued growing, a battle raging within its bark. Roots turned black before they withered and pearly branches sprouted instead.

Amani closed his eyes. The Istoria Arbor towered easily over all other trees in the forest, shining like a brilliant beacon. When the intense glow had faded, he opened his eyes again. With his mouth agape, Amani gazed at the thick branches, how white leaves with golden veins unfurled, releasing millions of floating lights over Eventide. An anguished cry wailed through the air before it died away.

There were no shadows tainting the tree anymore.

He reached out to the gentle, sparkling dust, so familiar to his sight. He smiled when Eventide was gleaming with lights once more. He laughed to celebrate Keiana's brave and selfless victory, but grew solemn when he looked at her staff in his hands. The kristars sparked when he ran his fingers over them, but the light inside of it seemed to gleam with magic.

He blinked upon hearing faint voices whisper.

All I ask of you, is to tell my story. Can you do that?

"Istoria Arbor, Keiana's Tree of Stories, the First of the Mythica." He took a deep breath and put his hand on the shining tree. It felt alive with energy, brimming at his touch. "I will fulfill my promise to you. I swear, on my life, your story will be told." A warmth spread from his hand through his body, as though he were enveloped in a tender embrace.

As the twinkling lights descended to the earth, traveling with the wind, they sought other chosen ones, other Mythicas to whisper their stories to.

Amani was one of them.

These new Storytellers learned more about the powers of the light, teaching others through their stories and wisdom about the world and the endless battle between light and darkness. Thus, the knowledge from one generation could be passed on to the next.

Keiana's story was always the first story told. Her legacy was never forgotten.

Over the years, the wise Mythicas were revered, as each story they told made another leaf grow on the branches of Istoria Arbor, keeping the floating lights burning brightly.

Though the Mythicas still exist, they are few, but persist confidently in their traditions, telling the stories of the past to hopefully one day guide their people toward a brilliant future, as Keiana once had.

CHAPTER 6

Like a Moth to the Flame

Hovering over the old woman's palm, Istoria Arbor shone with the radiance of the sun. Some of the leaves—which were black just a few moments ago—now glowed a bright white as I finished penning down the story she told me.

While I only had the skill of writing stories, this proclaimed Mythica told the story of Keiana and Istoria Arbor with the use of the light. I studied the floating specks, still in disbelief that stories were the reason for their everlasting burning.

Who would have thought stories had that kind of power?

"I saw a tree before I fell. Was it the Istoria Arbor? I could go and see it—if I wanted to?" I asked, wondering how long it would have taken me to reach it if I hadn't fallen.

The woman smiled, waving her hand to disperse the image. "One can certainly try, Wanderer."

"Why do you say that as if you know I won't be able to find it?"

"Very few do." She looked at my hands before her eyes shifted to the dragon who still rested on my shoulder. The creature blinked and nodded at her, answering a question only it could hear. It leapt off of me and back into her arms.

"Are you satisfied with my story, Wanderer? Will it do for your collection?"

I scrambled to nod in gratitude. "Quite! Thank you for sharing that story with me." A moment of silence passed between us and I shifted in my seat. "If you don't mind me asking though, why do you want me to tell this particular story to others? Is there a reason for it?"

"No more than my desire to share stories from my world to yours. I am a Mythica, after all."

The woman smiled at me, though something seemed off about her face. The invisible veil I thought I had seen before seemed like it shifted, as if it were a mask and her true face was fighting to reveal itself. I felt suspicious, but I couldn't pinpoint why.

"Then, at least may I know your name? So I can credit this story to you." This earned me a wholehearted laugh from the woman. Even the black dragon seemed to snicker.

"No need for that. Consider me a traveler who simply likes to tell people stories." She winked at me, but to my ears, she sounded less like a woman, and a lot more like a man just now. Had I been concentrating so much that I was starting to imagine things? Was she some kind of spirit?

"It was an honor to have enjoyed your company," she said as she rose from the boulders, groaning and supporting her back. "But I fear we must away. You have other paths to tread yourself."

"Oh, yes, of course..." I looked around and was suddenly reminded by the fact that I had no idea which way to head to next.

"Before you leave, do you think you could tell me which way to go? I would love to explore some more, but something tells me I have to keep on moving. Except, I don't know which path to take to move me forward."

"Have no fear, Wanderer, you'll find your way," the woman said, turning around to leave.

I still had many questions I wanted to ask, but I guess whatever task she thought she needed to fulfill had been done. I suppose it was my task now to take her story and move on with my own journey.

A frightening loud roar ripped through the air. So much so it made my ears ring. The ground shook and I tried to keep my balance steady.

"What was that?" I asked, breathlessly. I had never heard a sound like that before. It left my bones quivering, my heart still thudding like it wanted to burst through my ribcage.

The woman, on the other hand, simply turned to gaze at the sky. She gave me another one of those mysterious smiles.

"Oh, forgive me, I thought you would have realized by now that this world is not unfamiliar to dragons roaming the skies." She casually gestured at the black dragon perched on her shoulder.

I, on the other hand, felt like someone had just smacked me across the face. "What?" I squeaked, before clearing my throat. "That is to say—*what*?! There are dragons here? I mean, actual, life-sized dragons that spit fire, not like that little skink?" I earned a hiss from the black dragon, and the Mythica nodded.

"Of course. They come in all shapes and sizes. A few do spit fire, others have different abilities."

Stunned at her easy explanation, I couldn't help but scoff. "Well, why didn't you tell me a story about a dragon instead?" I asked, feeling jittery and excited at the same time. Imagine that, dragons, real! All my life I had always wanted to meet a life-sized dragon.

The woman tilted her head at me in amusement, a strange glint in her eyes as she regarded me. "Because, Wanderer, *that* story is not mine to tell. It hasn't started yet, but I suppose it'll give you more cause to visit again."

An invisible mask shifted over her face, something I couldn't put my finger on. The snow white hood she placed over her head covered her face now, and I wondered if it was still a woman under there, or someone else.

"Who are you?" I asked again.

"I am no one of importance," she said. "Merely a humble traveler that likes to meddle in a game of fate now and again." She bowed before me, eyes shifting towards the sky again when the roar of a dragon sounded for a second time.

"Best be on your way, Wanderer. Dragons love the scent of new flesh." She chuckled as she walked away. I had my eyes glued to the sky, anxiously and hopefully searching, trying to catch a glimpse of the mighty beast. However, when the dragon roared a third time, the warning of the Mythica rang clearly in my head, and I made myself scarce.

How foolishly I rushed away, only later finding out that dragons were not at all as vicious as they appeared... The woman had been right about that. The greatest story that will grow from Istoria Arbor will have to wait for another time.

Again, I found myself roaming an unfamiliar forest, unsure where to go and unsure where I'd end up this time. I kept an eye on the sky, just in case a dragon flew by, but each time I looked up, I thought about the cliff I had fallen from. By all accounts, I shouldn't have survived a fall that high, but there was a magic in this place, flowing around me.

I was far away from home, though the journey to reach it was filled with apprehensive excitement.

Knowing better than to let my guard down in a foreign place, I strode on, hoping to encounter something that might help me find the right path to choose. Would I find more stories to collect? More tales to fill my notebook with?

I looked around, at the soft floating lights and dim shadows in the deeper parts of the woods. A chill ran down my spine thinking about the story the Mythica told me. Would this forest still have demons lingering in the darkness?

I don't want to find out...

It was only after walking for the best part of the day that I realized how abandoned the forest was. How quiet it had grown.

During my earlier journey, the birds had sung their songs in the trees, the bees buzzing from one flower to another. The woods had creaked and crackled, pine cones falling from the high branches as the breeze swept past the dancing leaves. But here, there was no sound. Not even a gust of wind.

The silence grew deafening with each step I took, and just as I thought to turn around and find a different way, the cocoon of silence broke.

Twigs snapped further away and I frowned in confusion when I caught the scent of fire. An orange glow appeared in front of me, the fire surrounded by a circle of impressively tall sequoia trees. The flames flickered and sparked, dancing to a silent song.

While I wasn't cold or weary, I was still drawn by the fire. The colors were so warm and so bright amongst all this green.

A part of me knew the woods had fallen quiet for a reason, and I should be on my guard, but another part of me was driven by insatiable curiosity. After assuring myself there was no one dangerous around, I walked toward the fire.

The first thing I felt was the temperature. Though the fire was small, it radiated enough heat to warm an entire house. The bizarre thing was, the fire didn't appear to need any real firewood to stay lit. It was hovering just above the ground. When the wind blew some small branches toward it, the wood crackled instantaneously, though the flames remained airborne.

"How does this work?" I muttered, blinking when I noticed a small vial of liquid on a tree stump near the fire. It looked so out of place I had to investigate. I picked up the tiny vial and read the label.

"'Pour me'," I read, chuckling to myself. "Pour you, where?" An odd tingling rushed over my fingers. Frowning, I turned the vial the other way and nearly dropped it in shock.

Over the fire, the label read.

"How in the world...?"

My hand trembled and I shifted my gaze to the floating fire. I looked around again, just to make sure there wasn't anyone nearby, that this wasn't some kind of trick that would get me into trouble.

Shutting my eyes and doing my utmost best to restrain myself, I put the vial back down. Having read enough books and seen enough movies, I knew mysterious vials containing mysterious liquid, labeled with commands, were a recipe for trouble. Something I could definitely do less with at the moment.

"Let's just continue the journey, shall we?" I murmured to myself, looking at the giant sequoias surrounding the fire like guardians.

As I chose a path to follow, a creeping sense of foreboding

overwhelmed my senses. My ears twitched. I turned around, jumping with a shriek.

The person who had snuck up on me out of nowhere, copied my movements and shrieked louder than I did, gazing at me in sheer shock with wide, bright eyes, as if I was the one who had startled him. We stood frozen in front of each other, studying one another from head to toe.

This new person truly put the 'strange' in stranger. His eyes were wide with bewilderment, but they were framed by a painted half-mask drawn on his sheet-white face. His lips were a ruby red, slightly parted to mimic my own shock. If I didn't know any better, I would've assumed he was a jester.

Where did he come from?

I looked behind him where the fire still burned and it amazed me to see how the stranger's hair was nearly the same color of the flames, as if he had emerged from the fire itself.

"Um, hello," I finally said after a long and stunned silence.

The man blinked, seemingly surprised I could speak. He lurched forward, his face inches from mine, despite the fact I was leaning away from him.

"Who are you?" he asked, a look of suspicion in his eyes.

Not wanting to give away who I was to some strange man, I thought about what the Mythica had called me. Jutting out my chin I said, "I am a Wanderer, a collector of stories."

I'm sure I could have said it with more confidence and conviction, but it seemed to do the trick. The clown-like man gasped softly, taking a step back.

"A collector of stories?" He eyed me up and down. "I knew a collector of stories once, nasty fellow! You're not him, are you?"

Astonished, I waited for the man to burst out laughing, claiming he was joking, but he didn't. In fact, I had never seen anyone regard me this seriously before.

"I am not him," I said slowly, causing the man's grave demeanor to change to one of relief and relaxation.

"Ah, good, that's a load off." He grinned at me, spinning a scepter I hadn't noticed before. I took a step back to create some distance between us, uncertain how to respond to someone who obviously wasn't one hundred percent 'there'.

He kept staring at me with that grin on his face. I cleared my throat.

"Who are you?"

He seemed delighted I had asked the question.

"Well, Collector of Stories, I am lost," he said, moving around as though he was searching for something.

"You're...lost? You mean your name is Lost, or, are you lost?" I asked, but he merely continued pacing, pointing at me.

"Yes!"

I could only stare at him, baffled.

"I'm looking for someone, see, but you're not it, Collector of Stories, no, no, not the one," he muttered, mostly to himself, "and yet, the one." He mused thoughtfully for a second before wandering further through the area.

I took a deep breath, looking for the quickest way to escape from this rambling lunatic.

"All right..." I backed away. "Good luck with finding whomever it is you're looking for." I swiftly turned around.

"You're leaving?" He sounded genuinely upset. His eyes shone with worry and his shoulders slumped.

"Um, yes. Uh, you see, I've stories to collect."

A frown appeared on his face. "You'd leave me alone here in the dark, so you may chase your stories? They're very elusive, you know, and not nearly as lost as I am. They know where they are so they'll never be able to find you, since you don't know where you are now, do you?"

My mind spun as I tried to understand his rhetoric. "W-well, I suppose that is true, but I do know I'm here, with you. I'm sure that must count for something."

"Ah, quite right you are, Collector of Stories," he exclaimed, before gasping. "Does that mean that I am your story?" He gasped even louder. "You're not here to collect *me*, are you?"

I shook my head at this confusing man, trying to keep my wits about me.

"How can I collect you? You're not a story..."

"Exactly! I am lost, which is precisely why you should never leave lost things alone in the dark." He nodded, as if he'd made some brilliant point. My mind spun.

"Well, if I did leave you, it still wouldn't be dark." I paused a moment to watch him stopping to sniff a tree and lick it. I shook my head. "There's a fire here, so you shouldn't be afraid of the dark."

The man gasped again and ran toward me in a panic, only to hide behind my back.

"Fire? Where?" he asked, peeking over my shoulder.

Gobsmacked, I pointed at the fire in the middle of the circle of trees.

He squeaked in fear. "Fire! Quick, you should douse that! Have you never heard of Forest Fire? Nasty things, they roam about in the woods, just blazing around like this one! Terrible! Hurry, douse it!"

"It's just a fire. Why are you so afraid of it?" I asked.

"Fire is treacherous. It doesn't lead you, unless it leads you astray. Now, hurry, put it out! There's water in that vial!" The man rushed to the tree stump where the vial sat.

"Wait! You can't just douse the fire. You didn't start it, maybe someone kept it lit for a reason!"

"No matter, I'm ending it!" the man said, his shaky hands struggling to keep the vial steady. As he approached the flame, he opened the vial and was about to pour the contents over it when the flames crackled and popped, causing him to shriek again and hide behind me instead.

"You do it!" His plea was so urgent, he pushed the vial into my hand.

"Will you leave me be if I do this?"

The man nodded vigorously. "Hurry!"

I exhaled deeply, moving toward the fire, hoping not to invoke any kind of anger by dousing this mysterious flame.

The feeling of unease crept back into my skin. I read the words on the vial and shook my head. "I can't do this. This feels off."

"That's because you have to pour it *out*, like so!"

Before I knew what was happening, the kooky stranger grabbed my hand and spilled the liquid over the fire. It started smoking.

"Well, I hope you're satisfied," I said. The smoke thickened, spreading itself further and further. "What's happening?" My eyes were stinging, clouding my vision.

"Oh no, I warned you the fire is treacherous, Collector of Stories," the man said.

I coughed to clear my lungs. "But you're the one who told me to do it! You were the one that turned my hand over!" I wasn't sure why I thought arguing with the man would make any difference.

"Well, serves you right, listening to someone who's lost."

The smoke thickened into a black fog. I couldn't even see through it. The gray billows swirled around like a vortex, surrounding us. I grunted, my throat burning, my eyes watering.

"I can't see!"

"Well, to be fair, no one could have seen this coming, don't be too harsh on yourself."

"You're insane!" I tried to scream, before coughs racked through my body.

"Ah, am I insane again? Wonderful, that means I'm not lost anymore!" He clapped his hands together, and caught me as I sank to my knees, the heat of the smoke and fire making me feel weak.

"You, on the other hand..." His voice barely kept me awake as my consciousness slipped away.

"I suppose now, you're just as lost as I was..."

part three

Fire

CHAPTER 7
the Seeker

With shadows dancing and crawling on earth,
A hero is sought, but no word on his birth.
Can light find the way in a world that is lost?
*Is a **Quill** the way to uncross what has been crossed?*

"**M**m..."
I woke up with the residue of smoke still burning in my lungs. Groaning, I swatted my hands around to get rid of the remnants of the thick vapor, gasping for fresh air. Rubbing my eyes, I scanned my environment. The smoke eventually cleared but it took a while for the hazy cloud to leave my peripherals.

How long had I been knocked out?

The first thing I noticed was that the fire had very much gone out. The circle of sequoias was nowhere to be seen, either. Rubbing the back of my head, I remembered hearing a voice and I searched for the crazy man that caused all of this mess. I didn't know what he was thinking, but reciting weird poetry while I was choking on smoke was not the proper way to help someone.

A cold sense of dread gripped my heart when I noticed I was abandoned. I found myself lost in another new environment. The entirety of the woods seemed to have changed.

"Where am I now?" I muttered to myself, taking tentative steps forward. The woodlands from before had been rather glum and quiet, but this forest was a lot more colorful. It was like I'd been transported to a floral paradise. The grass grew tall here in various shades of green, bending in the wind. Flowers bloomed in lush bushes and near the feet of tree groves. Not one of them looked the same, their petals seemingly splashed by rainbows.

Berries and odd-looking fruits hung heavy from thick branches, but I couldn't identify them. Could you eat fruit pulsating with golden juices?

A terrifying growl ripped through the tranquil air and rosy blushes dusted my cheeks. I patted my stomach, my mouth watering. Those fruits looked delicious and I hadn't eaten for a while.

I moved toward one of the trees and carefully touched the glittering bark. As if responding to my touch, one of the branches bowed low enough for me to grasp a plump, purple-pink fruit. Shaped like a butterfly, I thought it would have flown away the moment I touched it, but the fruit was smooth and heavy with juices.

Totally willing to risk food poisoning, I carefully bit into it. The fruit was surprisingly soft and a bomb of flavors erupted in my mouth, dancing on my tongue. The cool and refreshing juice was like a rain shower in the spring, but the taste was savory, like baked goods made during the autumn.

I must've hummed my approval a bit too loudly, as a flock of silver-winged birds had suddenly shot up to the sky, dashing past me.

"Whoa..."

It gave me some relief to hear signs of life around me. The

whistling of birds were like individual little melodies; pure, clear tunes that sounded like songs. The leaves moved and rustled in the light breeze, the soft chimes of bells rippling from them. The sounds I heard around me were the sounds of the wood singing and breathing. It made absolutely no sense, but I felt like the forest here was actually alive.

I took another careful step forward, taking in the fresh scent of honeysuckle in the air. Brightly colored flowers lay strewn across the forest floor, gentle sparkles emitting from them. They resembled the floating lights I had seen earlier, except these sparkled beautifully in the low-hanging sun and gave off a sweet, fresh smell. When I gently touched one of the flowers, its petals lit up briefly and played a soft note like that of a piano.

My moment of wonder was interrupted when I heard something heavy dragging across the earth.

I turned my head at the noise and startled when the same sound came from the opposite side. I jumped when I thought I saw the root of a tree move by itself.

"Hello? Is someone there?"

Why would I expect an answer if someone was purposefully hiding from me? Rolling my eyes at my own stupidity, I gazed around the woods, searching for more movement, seeking the man I had spoken to before. He had to be around here somewhere as well, right? He was engulfed by the smoke the same way I was.

Then again, that didn't have to mean a thing. He had appeared out of nowhere. It wouldn't be such a surprise if he managed to disappear the same way, too.

"All right," I said to myself, attempting to get a grip on the situation. "How difficult can it be to keep walking? I'm sure I'll end up somewhere..."

But where?

Deciding not to dwell on it, I grabbed the straps of my backpack and started trekking. The sweet air of the forest did me some good, and I luckily didn't seem to suffer too much from inhaling all that smoke—as long as I didn't think back to it. The memory made me cough again.

While I had no idea where I was going, it was great to be on the move. The sun was hanging low in the sky, but I couldn't tell whether it was setting or rising. I wonder how long I had been journeying. I wasn't tired at all. Of course, who knows how long I had been out cold after inhaling so much smoke? Still, I didn't feel fatigued. Could that be some kind of positive effect from traveling through these worlds?

These worlds...

I was starting to learn that things around here seemed to have a natural, albeit unconventional, way of moving things forward, almost as if something was planning my path out for me. I had never been someone to question the things that were happening to me, so I certainly wasn't going to start, but how was I going to explain everything I've seen thus far? Why, of all people, had *I* been chosen to go on this adventure? Why was it so important that *I* write down the stories told here?

I thought back to the Mythica, how she was so adamant I share her story with others. How had she called them—*Wayfarers*? She had called me a *Wanderer*... Was there a difference? Did Wanderers collect stories to share with Wayfarers who would be able to travel through the worlds of these stories as they read about them? How did darkness and light tie in to that?

I reminisced about the voice I heard when I was a child. How it spoke about my light being too weak. Considering I was walking through a magnificent forest, and have seen some incredible things, I guess that light the voice spoke about was finally strong enough. Whatever the reason, I was still thrilled to be on this journey, and I was absolutely convinced that if I was chosen for this adventure, I certainly had the skills to get myself back home *eventually*.

Taking a deep breath, and feeling quite satisfied with myself, I gazed at my environment with utmost appreciation. When the wind rustled the leaves, they shimmered from green to gold and silver. The colorful flora seemed to bloom as I walked by. I even smiled at the faces that seemed etched on tree barks, touching one in particular that had a round, bulging nose. I must have walked for another hour or so, still marveling at the sights around me.

This truly was a beautiful forest. Never had I seen the colors so bright, breathed air so fresh. Even the plants seemed happy. I grinned as my imagination ran off with me, and I patted the bulging nose of a tree as I passed by—*wait*.

I took a closer look at the face in the tree, narrowing my eyes at it.

Didn't I see this tree before?

Looking around the environment with a new sense of alarm, a sheen of sweat covered my body as realization smacked me hard across the face.

"You've got to be kidding me!" My voice echoed through the woods as I saw a trail of footsteps in the dirt in front of me. I set my feet next to them for comparison and the blood drained from my body.

I've been walking in circles all this time?!

Groaning, I recognized the spot I woke up in. I could even still smell the remnants of smoke through the honeysuckle.

How could I get lost? I literally walked a straight line, how could I have circled back?

Panic frayed my nerves, and I remembered the strange rhyme

I heard before regaining consciousness. I knew I heard that voice, and I knew it could only mean that stranger was here somewhere as well. As much as I loathed it, he was the only thing I could think of who might be able to help me find my way. I resented the irony of suddenly needing to find him when I wanted nothing more but to escape from him earlier on.

Ridiculous. Why should I try to find him? He's the one that put me in this mess in the first place!

I bit my lip.

Maybe that's why he's the only one who could get me out of here...

The warm and bright atmosphere of the woods swiftly turned sinister. Flashes of shadows flitted past the trees, lingering mist crept over the earth. There was something hidden behind the shine and beauty of the forest, something crawling at me.

I had been too enchanted by the urge to explore. I shouldn't have been so careless.

"This is not good." I had no idea which way to go and couldn't find the crazy man anywhere. I decided to move on, no longer feeling safe standing out in the open. I purposely chose a different path, taking turns and paying close attention to my surroundings.

If there was a reason I was here, I couldn't guess what it was right now. I still felt like I was walking in circles, but at least the environment changed around me. Could I make it without the weird clown-man after all?

"Whoa." I halted in my tracks, rudely awakened from my thoughts. I gazed at a massive... Well, to be frank, I wasn't quite sure what I was looking at.

A shudder rippled through my body from head to toe as I leaned back to gawk at the giant contraption.

Looming over me like a mountain, stood a giant egg-shaped dome.

It was covered in vines and moss, wild flowers and roots, coiling over each other. Thick lianas kept the edifice erect, though part of me feared it would topple over anyway if the wind blew a little too hard.

What was a thing like this doing in the middle of the forest?

I was so lost taking in the impressive structure that, for a second time, I didn't notice someone sneaking up on me. Movement caught the corner of my eye, and I turned around in time to face it. The shriek flew from my mouth when the person next to me jumped as well.

With a hand over my chest I pointed at the red-headed stranger from before. "You! Will you stop scaring me like that?"

"Me? *You're* the one scaring me!"

I looked at him in disbelief. "You were the one who snuck up on me— again!"

He frowned deeply. "Have we met?"

My jaw dropped. And here I thought finding him would bring relief. *Idiot!*

I sighed in exasperation after mentally scolding myself. "No, we haven't met. If you'll excuse me, I'll be on my way," I said, since it didn't seem I'd made much of an impression on him to begin with.

"Are you lying to me?" he asked, following as I walked away.

"Yes, I am, but something tells me that when you disappear and return again, you won't remember who I am anyway." I didn't have the patience or the time for this. How could I have thought he could help me out?

"That makes sense," he mused. Then he jumped, out of the blue. "Wait!" He moved to stand in front of me, blocking my path. "You're not going in there, are you?" He gestured at the large dome.

"Is there a reason why I shouldn't?"

"I forgot"—he scratched his head—"but bad things are inside there—or was it that a bad man wanted to collect things from it?"

As he pondered nonsensically to himself again, I moved past him to go see for myself.

"No, wait, you shouldn't go in there without a proper guide, mad things are afoot!"

"The only mad thing here, is you." A wide grin appeared on his face as I shook my head at him. "I thought you said you were looking for someone? You even explicitly told me I wasn't them, so why do you keep following me?"

"I am looking for someone, indeed! A collector of stories!"

"*I'm* a collector of stories," I said, wondering why I even bothered.

"Are you? You're not the nasty one, are you? I didn't like him," he said, as if apprehensive.

I groaned. "I am a woman! We've had this conversation before!"

He gazed at me as if I was the one who had lost their marbles. "Have we? Oh well, in that case you're not the person I'm looking for," he said with a grin.

"You've really lost your mind, haven't you?" I took a deep, steady breath. "You need help."

He gasped at this, grabbing me by my shoulders and nodding fervently. "I do. I do need help," he agreed, biting down on his ruby lips, eyes glazing over and moving from side to side. "I think I know where I can get help!" He giggled before grabbing my hand and dragged me toward the very thing he had warned me not to enter.

"Hold on! You said I shouldn't go in there!"

"Oh, rightly, you shouldn't! The C'Ovo is a very dangerous place— unless you have a guide." His eyes gleamed as I started to wonder whether he was fooling me, or whether he truly was out of his mind.

"The *ko-vo*?" I repeated, looking up at the egg-shaped dome.

"What's in the *ko-vo*?" My curiosity burst through, shoving rational reasoning out of the way.

There was something somber and grave about the strange man now as he faced me. "Pain. Suffering. Lost things," he said softly before sighing, looking down at my hand he was still holding.

"You are a collector of stories, you say." He looked at me. His eyes shimmered with a glint of something odd, something sharply intelligent. "Perhaps you can collect things that are lost, as well, or collect lost things here." He blinked, smiling brightly at me again. "Do you own a quill, Collector of Stories?"

"A quill? I have a pen." I showed it to him and he cooed.

"Wonderful, this will do! Make sure to write down everything we collect. Perhaps we won't be lost anymore! Off we go!" he announced with a cheer, tugging at my arm before I even had the sense to argue. He left me with little else to do but to follow him inside the dome, with naught but a pen as a weapon to defend myself from danger.

CHAPTER 8
the tale of C'Ovo

Fire is a dangerous monstrosity.

Fire destroys without mercy, it spreads without respecting boundaries, killing all that dare stand in its way. Out of all the harrowing fires that exist in the world, there is one kind that is the most devastatingly destructive of all. It is all-consuming, ever-blazing and unquenchable. Nothing could be more insidious than this: the Fire of Love.

Yech! Love... Such messy business, so dramatic, so exhausting!

How much pain and suffering has love caused? Honestly, who falls in love willingly?

No one!

It happens unexpectedly, and before you truly realize what befell you, the Fire of Love has started its merciless carnage, setting any lovestruck fool utterly, and relentlessly, ablaze.

Pity those consumed by the Flames of Love! Those poor fools will find no solace here. In this world, where madness is considered a disease, how can anything good come for those madly in love? Anything touched by fire will ultimately get burned, especially in this realm, which was once the playground of the Gods.

The world nourished itself. F'Airies flew through the skies, breathing life into the world, controlling the weather to their own whims. Earth Fays tended to the fertile lands, and Water Sprites fed all that grew and lived in the woods.

Fire demons did not belong there. Their blazing brilliance did not fit within the luminosity of the world. It burned too hotly, too fiercely. Their light was one tainted with destructive darkness. Smoke riddled the air where their flames burned, the lands scorched and barren under their feet. And water... Such a peculiar relationship fire has with water. Water kept fire at bay, like true protectors, guarding all of creation against the annihilation brought by these wretched fire demons.

Why one of those evil, malicious creatures would risk creeping near the banks of a majestic lake was a curious mystery indeed.

Do not be fooled by her alluring appearance as she stalks the edges with frightening precision. Do not be seduced by her big eyes of brilliant ember, smoldering and gazing about in childlike curiosity. Beware her long flowing hair, made of blazing flames. This deity was pure fire. She breathed blistering heat, her touch burned like no other. Scorch marks were left in her wake. Her shimmering red and orange skin would soon be doused like a burning sun setting in the cool horizon.

"Demon!"

"Temptress!"

Though Te'Kala shielded her ears from the accusations, the words still cut through her heart. Confused and running from those who meant her harm, the fire deity finally found a quiet place near a lake to be left alone. All she had done was attempt to befriend some woodland critters, before a small group of Earth Fays drove her away, fearful that disaster would come for them. Was it her fault the sticks and stones they had thrown at her caught on fire or bounced off of her like smoldering coals? She never meant any harm.

If anything, when Te'Kala had woken up in the world of creation, she was so enamored and enchanted by it, she only desired to create as well. While she soon found out there seemed to be no place for the likes of her in this new realm, the longing to create burned only stronger inside of her.

While walking near the tranquil lake, admiring the glint of the sun reflecting off the mirrored surface, Te'Kala reminisced the times she tried her hand at creating. In moments of solitude, she would create flowers of fire, to be admired alongside the flowers she so loved, but her fire flowers ended up consuming others in bright flames, nearly setting the entire forest alight.

There was also a time when she attempted to create a tree of fire from one already standing in the woods, but it went up in a flare of flames from the roots to the highest leaves. It blazed like a beautiful, brilliant balefire. For the briefest moment, the Fire Tree stood proud and shining, until the first branches broke and soon nothing was left but a pile of ash. It served as a solemn headstone the winds would soon scatter. Despite her best efforts, her creations simply didn't take.

Te'Kala's attempts to create were rather amusing, but the fire deity was ridden with sorrow. If she could cry, she would have, but her tears fell from inside her heart instead.

Perhaps the stories she heard others tell about her kind were true after all. Te'Kala looked at her hands, at the flames she was able to produce with a simple thought. She let them glide over her skin, smiling to herself at the dancing figures. Was this not a form of creation? It might not be something permanent, but it certainly wasn't destructive.

Her heart stung and the dancing flames dispersed. She shouldn't have been thinking about these trivial things, but she couldn't help herself. There had to be more to this life than how she had led it so far.

She glanced around her, admired the glittering leaves rustling on golden branches, breathed in the sweet scent of honeysuckle which she could nearly taste on her tongue. Te'Kala even appreciated the beauty of the lake before her, how serene and inviting the blue water seemed. A ripple ran through her body, her blazing hair sparking at the sensation. She wondered how many of her kind were sent to a state of *unexisting* by that strange liquid, evaporated into smoke and ash.

"And they call me dangerous," Te'Kala whispered to herself, briefly leaning forward to glance at her reflection. The blue of the lake played with the orange and red glow she emitted. She might have thought the sight beautiful, were she not aware of how dangerous the water could be.

Bubbles formed on the water's surface, disrupting the mirrored glaze. When they popped, Te'Kala leaned back, stepping away from the lake as it started rippling and moving. She hugged her arms together, a gasp escaping her lips.

Something broke through the surface.

Roused by fear, Te'Kala shot a ball of fire at the entity in the water.

Her eyes widened when a pale hand shot out to catch it, the fiery blaze hissing as it doused, reducing the flaming ball into a metallic lump of rock.

"Quite a powerful arm you have." Someone chuckled as the water receded from the figure's form.

Te'Kala stood frozen, her gaze still lingering on the lump of rock.

Her fire meant nothing to this creature. A mere flick of the hand and the water could consume her, reduce *her* into a lump of stone. Her breath hitched and she quickly turned to flee.

"No, wait! I didn't mean to frighten you, please, I won't harm you."

Te'Kala scoffed and kept moving.

"I'm sorry. I thought someone like you would be tired of running away all the time. I suppose I was wrong."

The fire deity knew better than to be swayed by the words of the stranger, especially a Water Sprite, but she still found herself halting, curiosity prickling her senses. Was this a ruse? Water Sprites were guardians of the woods, they were meant to destroy people like her.

Taking a deep breath, Te'Kala turned around to face the sprite, though she kept her distance. She was met—to her surprise—with a friendly smile.

"Hello."

The greeting sounded far too casual for Te'Kala's liking, especially accompanied by a pearly smile and vivacious dark blue eyes, framed by tiny iridescent shells. His hair was the color of kelp, a stark contrast to his pale skin.

Te'Kala kept watch over the droplets of water clinging to his body, falling gently onto the forest floor. He stepped carefully forward, placing the lump of rock on the ground.

"I won't harm you," he said, holding his hands in the air. "I saw you sitting at the bank of the lake—my lake"—he gestured a the water behind him—"and you seemed troubled so I thought I'd come to say hello."

Te'Kala merely frowned at him, keeping a healthy distance between her and the stranger.

"I was going to leave your lake. I didn't mean to trespass," she said. Her attempt to make her voice sound strong failed as the Water

Sprite nodded, unimpressed.

"You're free to stay as long as you like. Everyone who visits my lake is welcome here, provided they have no ill intentions, of course." His chuckle bubbled effortlessly out of his throat, as if kindness came easy to him, but something in the statement made Te'Kala's blood boil.

"Is that why you emerged from your shelter? Because you saw a fire demon with ill intentions that could set everything here ablaze?" A black ring appeared around her feet, the ground scorching as her anger grew.

"Calm down. I just thought you were... Well, you looked lonely, that's all." His voice was soothing, but Te'Kala was not fooled.

"I'm not lonely and I am calm! Why would a Water Sprite concern himself with someone like me?" The black ring around her grew wider and Te'Kala realized too late that her temper was causing small flowers to catch fire. She moved forward in an attempt to stop it from spreading, accidentally brushing against a tree which started to burn. Te'Kala startled and in her panic, she moved back, brushing up against blades of grass and bushes. She sunk down on the ground to avoid touching anything else.

She squealed when water slithered around her, extinguishing the flames with a sizzle. The water splashed from the burning bark and a few drops fell on her shoulder. Te'Kala hissed and covered the wound with her hand, watching the streams of water flow back toward the Water Sprite. She ducked further away from him when he stood before her.

She was certain this was the end. She would perish in a world she never belonged to. Te'Kala shut her eyes, wincing and waiting for her demise. When she wondered why the Water Sprite prolonged her suffering, she found him knelt in front of her, an eyebrow raised.

"Ah yes," he said, "I see you are the epitome of calmness."

Te'Kala frowned at the smirk on his face. "You're not going to douse me?"

Something glimmered in his eyes before he sighed and shook his head. "You've met my kind before, I assume?"

Taken aback, Te'Kala sputtered to reply. "I—well, I mean—"

"It's all right, there's no need for you to explain. I understand. My kind hasn't really been courteous to your kind, have they?"

Unsure whether he expected her to answer, Te'Kala only watched him as he got up on his webbed feet and walked toward a nearby tree. Confused, she decided to wait and see what he'd do next.

He plucked a peculiar-looking flower from the root of a tree. It was shaped like a star, with petals in various colors. He crushed it between his fingers and black juice spilled from it before turning into liquid gold. It swirled and shaped itself as though alive, staying neatly contained in the sprite's hands. Te'Kala scurried away when he brought the liquid near her injured shoulder.

"Stay away! If you mean to douse me, do so immediately. Don't poison me with whatever *that* is," she said fiercely, fire flaring from her body.

"This is called Fool's Gold." He sounded gentle when he spoke, like someone soothing a child. "This liquid will heal anything, except for death, heartache and madness." He waited before approaching, a questioning look in his eyes.

Te'Kala shook her head, trying to understand the stranger's motives. Why would he help her?

"I'm made of fire," she finally said, "liquid of any kind is harmful to me."

"Not this one. I assure you."

"I have no reason to trust you." Te'Kala leaned away from him, attempting to read his expression. She had learned to recognize fear on the first day she woke up in the new world. She saw the expression on every face she met, but this Water Sprite did not show any hints of fear. He looked calm, patient. She didn't quite like how he smiled at her, but thus far, he hadn't treated her with any hostility.

"I have no reason to hurt you," he said, interrupting her thoughts.

"But I'm a fire demon."

"Does that mean you should be denied the right to exist in this world?"

Te'Kala blinked. She hadn't expected to be this tongue-tied, in front of a Water Sprite, no less. The silence falling between them was prolonged as they watched each other, waiting for someone to move first. Finally, her protective flames simmered down, her eyes glancing at the Fool's Gold.

Remember what he is, Te'Kala...

She swallowed. "Who are you?"

A small smile flashed across the stranger's face before he straightened. "I am Letheon. What may I call you?"

"I am Te'Kala," she said in a similar fashion, wincing when her shoulder stung.

"Te'Kala..." He repeated her name as if he tried to taste it. "May I offer you help, Te'Kala? That looks like it hurts." He pointed at her shoulder, holding the Fool's Gold at the ready. "If you would like to leave after this, you are free to do so. I only mean to help."

Taking a deep breath, she exposed her shoulder to him. "I can still attack you," she said in warning.

This made Letheon laugh. "Yes, your fireball was quite effective."

"The flames may douse in your hand, but the molten rocks can still hit your head!" Te'Kala retaliated, letting out a painful yelp when the Fool's Gold hissed on her wound.

"I'll keep that in mind." Letheon's smile never faltered and he took a step back to appraise the wound. "There. That wasn't too bad, was it?"

Te'Kala glared at him before rolling her shoulder, inspecting it. The pain was gone.

"How...?" She murmured to herself, prodding the skin to make sure she didn't feel the sting anymore. "It worked..."

"It left a small mark, though," Letheon said, inspecting her shoulder from afar. A darker shade of red splotched her skin. "It shouldn't leave any marks. Maybe I should put some more on?"

"No, it's fine, I don't mind," said Te'Kala, carefully standing. She brushed over her fiery hair. "Thank you, that was very kind. Where did you learn that?"

Letheon plucked a silver fruit from a bush nearby and peeled it methodically, revealing dark red orbs which he popped in his mouth. "My lake nourishes the lands surrounding it. I wouldn't be much of a Water Sprite if I didn't know what my water made grow."

"And your decision to help me? Are you expecting something in return?" she asked, frowning when Letheon looked displeased.

"Tell me, Te'Kala, are you someone who means to destroy everything in this world?"

The question made her bristle. "Of course not!"

"Me neither," Letheon said, before her temper flared up again. "I simply saw someone who looked lonely, and being familiar with that particular emotion, I thought I'd come up to meet you. That was my only intention." He walked back to the lake, still eating the dark red orbs. Te'Kala watched him and rubbed her shoulder.

"What would a Water Sprite know of loneliness? F'Airies dance on your lake, Earth Fays have probably never thrown rocks or sticks at you. You have no idea what it's like."

Letheon scratched the back of his neck, a soft blush fanning out over his cheeks. "Just because I seem to belong doesn't mean I do. Perhaps I'm different from other Water Sprites, and loneliness is the price one pays for that."

Te'Kala narrowed her eyes at him, absently rubbing her shoulder. "You've had time to think about this, haven't you?"

"Look around you. There's no one else here. All I had was time to contemplate." Letheon grinned and threw one of the orbs at her. Te'Kala caught it, panic rushing through her body when the orb was set alight. But instead of it blackening and turning to dust, the orb burned a pink smoke, giving off a creamy, delicate aroma.

"Go on, you can eat it," Letheon said.

Te'Kala sniffed at it before taking a bite. The orb oozed like lava in her mouth, but it invigorated her. The sweet taste sparked on her tongue and warmed her belly even more.

"Delicious, right?" Letheon smiled. "You won't find these fruits anywhere else. The bushes will only drink the water from my lake."

Still humming in approval, Te'Kala sat by the edge of the lake as Letheon slid into the water. "Why won't they drink other water? Is there a special kind of magic to it other lakes don't possess?" she asked.

"Of course," Letheon said with playful confidence. "Me."

Te'Kala smiled at his easygoing nature, and as the day flitted by, she realized it was the first time she had spent it comfortably with someone new.

When the stars began dotting the sapphire sky and her flames cast bigger shadows on the sand, Te'Kala stood. Letheon was a pleasant companion, something she had not expected when she first met him, and she felt rather reluctant to leave so soon.

"You can stay here, if you like. You won't have to leave. The sand won't catch fire and I'm sure it won't rain tonight," Letheon said, gliding in the water as he looked at her.

"I wish I could, but I can't." Te'Kala's throat tightened when she gazed at his eyes. "It was nice meeting you today, but I have to move on—for now."

"Will you be back?" he asked, stepping ashore.

"Maybe," she said, shuffling the sand with her feet. She wasn't quite sure what to make of the look of disappointment in his eyes.

"Well, just remember you're always welcome in this private sanctuary. When Earth Fays throw things at you again, you come back here and I'll make sure to keep them away."

"Really? You'd do that for a fire demon?" Te'Kala's hair swayed from side to side, her ember eyes glowing brighter as the night grew darker.

Remember what he is, Te'Kala.

Letheon grinned. "A fire *deity*. You're not a demon, Te'Kala, no matter what the rest of the world tells you."

"You are a strange one, Letheon," she said, smiling at him.

"Must be something in the water." The Water Sprite dove into the lake and emerged again, waving at her. "Take care, Te'Kala. I hope to see you again soon."

Te'Kala nodded. Running her fingers through her hair, she turned away to leave.

"Te'Kala, wait!"

She stopped and looked at him.

"I just recalled something. There's a part of the woods that doesn't quite feel right. I can't put my finger on it, but it's best to stay away, just to be safe— especially if there's a lake nearby. Not all Water Sprites are welcoming." Letheon smiled gently. Gleaming bubbles of water drifted up from his lake and popped, a drizzle of glitters cascading over him.

Te'Kala's hair flickered, the flames sparking slightly at the edges. She nodded and swallowed. "I'll be back," she said with determination, despite the nervous flutters pressing against her chest. She carefully moved past the trees and bushes, and disappeared from sight.

Cold was the night when Te'Kala moved through the forest, unperturbed by the icy chill and creeping darkness, so different from the woods near Letheon's lake. She thought of his kindness and of the orb she ate. She never thought about eating anything before, the air in the woods being enough to nourish her flames. It had been an odd yet pleasant sensation, though she wondered how Letheon knew the fruit wouldn't disintegrate in her hands. He acted so comfortably around her. Had he met someone like her before?

Te'Kala's flame shuddered as a cold breeze picked up and she arrived at another lake. Letheon's warning passed her mind and she hugged her arms, inspecting the change of scenery. Much larger than Letheon's lake, this body of water nourished the greater part of the forest. Water Sprites influenced the environment with their water, and this lake was connected to them all.

Well, not all of them...

Letheon's lake and the surrounding area had felt so light and warm. They were just like he was—a little strange, but familiar at the same time. The woods here were nothing like Letheon's. A pressing heaviness hung in the air here, a dizzying haze, thick with...magic.

Uneasiness crept over Te'Kala as she spotted an elegant figure hovering over the water. Not wanting to be spotted, Te'Kala sat amongst some boulders, keeping her head down.

The Water Sprite danced on the lake under the moonlight, her white, cascading hair swaying along with her graceful movements. Her eyes were an enchanting sea green, the dust of stars sprinkled on her cheeks.

Making herself as small as possible, Te'Kala contemplated running away, but she couldn't tear her gaze from the beautiful, bewitching sprite. The elegant figure swayed across the lake, her eyes glowing as water bubbled underneath her, hair floating behind her as if she danced underwater. Green mist flowed from her fingertips. The water coiled like serpents around her, blasting up to the sky before raining back down into glowing drops.

Te'Kala watched how the lake illuminated with magic. She took the moment to gaze at it, a twinge of sadness eating at her heart. The woods responded to that magic. It gave them life. She wasn't able to create like that, but maybe, one day, she could.

"You were gone a long time, beloved." The Water Sprite's voice chimed like bells, as delicate as water bubbles floating into the air.

Te'Kala cringed at the pet name, but she emerged from her hideout and walked onto the pearly white sands to meet the sprite. Lasirena always smiled at her, though the fire deity never quite knew why.

"I didn't mean to—"

"Didn't mean to, what? Sneak off and hope I wouldn't notice? Perhaps you didn't mean to leave me worrying sick about you, or did you not mean to get caught trying to sneak back?" Lasirena gestured with her slender fingers. Te'Kala jerked back. A trail of water followed Lasirena's movement, hovering over Te'Kala's skin without touching her.

"I'm sorry, I honestly didn't mean to worry you, but you were gone for most of the day and I thought I'd explore a little, that's all."

Te'Kala leaned away from the trail of water cascading inches before her. She could almost feel the icy cold touch of the liquid and her hand automatically moved to her shoulder.

"Explore?" Lasirena's eyes flitted to Te'Kala's shoulder, ribbons of water moving around her graceful figure. "How often must I tell you of the dangers beyond these woods, beloved? You know I would be terribly saddened if something bad happened to you."

"No, nothing bad happened," Te'Kala said, her voice muted. "I just got a little sidetracked."

"Sidetracked?" Lasirena had an odd way of speaking. She always sounded sweet, but there were moments when Te'Kala wasn't sure whether her words were as well.

"Y-yes..." She didn't know why she always stammered when she stood in front of Lasirena either. "There were some small animals I met in the woods while I was trying to—"

"Create?" Laughter filled the air. Lasirena shook her head. "I thought I told you, my love. Only once I feel you are ready can I bestow you the power to create. Not a moment sooner."

There. Her words were sweet but something jagged hid in her tone, a sharpness piercing through the skin.

"I know, but I only meant to try," Te'Kala said, watching Lasirena run her fingers through her white hair, spheres of water encircling her.

"And I suppose the Earth Fays injured your shoulder?"

Te'Kala's eyes widened, her flaming hair sparking in the wind. "Not precisely, I mean, I—" She shut her mouth when the water around Lasirena stopped moving. They seemed frozen, transforming into spikes as the sprite herself gazed at Te'Kala with her glowing sea green eyes.

"What aren't you telling me, beloved?"

Te'Kala's cheeks brightened, her flaming hair swaying. "Um, I just—"

"How far did you stray from these woods, exactly?"

Te'Kala fidgeted. "Not that far..." She peeked at Lasirena, who gazed right at her, an eyebrow raised. Finally, Te'Kala couldn't contain herself.

"I really didn't mean to stray as far as I did, but when I encountered those Earth Fays they drove me away, and then I came across another lake, and I lost track of time—I'm sorry." She took a deep breath, not as concerned over what Lasirena might think about her confession as she was excited having stumbled upon Letheon. "Oh, Lasirena, if you only you'd allow me to see more of this world. There's so much beauty in it. I know fire deities are frowned upon, but it's not as bad as you think. Not every creature living here wishes me ill will." She played with her hair a moment, her mind drifting to her encounter with Letheon. The interaction left her feeling warmer, her skin glowing softly.

Lasirena's mouth twitched, a darkness shrouding her eyes. "Where did all this talk come from? And what lake do you speak of?" She motioned at Te'Kala's shoulder, the spikes rushing around her form. "Did you encounter another Water Sprite? Where did you fi—Did they injure you?"

Taken aback by Lasirena's sudden loss of composure, Te'Kala was quick to answer. "No—well, technically, yes, but he didn't mean to, he was cleaning up the mess I accidentally caused."

Lasirena fell silent, unmoving before Te'Kala. Clouds veiled the glow of the moon, the wind passing by without a sound. The lights in the lake dimmed and were it not for Te'Kala, they would have been swallowed by the darkness.

"*He*?" Lasirena stood rigid, never once glancing away from

Te'Kala. "You encountered a male Water Sprite?"

Te'Kala swallowed. "I know I was reckless, but—"

"Other Water Sprites are dangerous, Te'Kala. They don't see you the way I do. You're lucky to have escaped with your life!"

"No, you don't understand, Letheon would never harm me. He's kind and attentive. We talked a lot, which was why I was so late to come back."

"Letheon?" Lasirena's movements were sharp and abrupt, her grace lost.

Te'Kala's fire burned a little stronger. She hid her smile behind her hair. "That's his name. We talked for hours and not once did he make me feel like I didn't belong." She curled a lock of flaming hair around her finger. "He made me feel welcome."

Something dark bubbled at the edge of the lake and Te'Kala jolted as the spikes splashed in the water. The sprite glided forward until they stood face to face.

"Has he made such an impression on you, beloved?" Lasirena's honeyed voice made Te'Kala shiver this time. "Were you so easily swayed by his otherworldly charm, hm?"

"I...He just..." Te'Kala's fire slunk back. "I thought we could be friends." Her stomach stung when Lasirena laughed.

"Oh, my dear, I hope you know better than to believe he would want to be friends with you."

"He was nothing but kind to me, and even asked me to stay." Her answer came out fiercer than intended as she stood her ground.

"My love, tell me you did not fall for his charade. You know you cannot trust other Water Sprites. They murder fire demons like you, they don't care to look beyond what you are."

Te'Kala pursed her lips. "But Letheon called me a deity, not a demon."

Lasirena sighed in exasperation. "And so you fall for his charms? A few sweet words are all it takes for you to forget everything I taught you about this world?" Her gentle voice grew louder. The lake trembled, the water rippling and waving. "Will you betray me and turn your back on me, after all I did for you?!"

Te'Kala fell back at Lasirena's outburst, breathing heavily as the sprite's fair face cracked like glass. Then, water slid over it, ridding her face neatly of the imperfections with a soft sizzle. Lasirena took a deep breath and Te'Kala held hers in.

"We belong to each other, beloved. I govern the lake and these woods, and you give it warmth. I won't let him take you from me. You understand, don't you?" Water rose from the lake again, like graceful sparrows taking flight. They flitted around Lasirena, who beamed warmly at Te'Kala again.

"I'm sorry I frightened you," she said. "Just the thought of someone using you, tempting you to fall for his guiles—I simply won't stand for it."

"What would make you think he would want to take me away?" Te'Kala asked, taking a small step back even though Lasirena had calmed down.

Lasirena's eyes gleamed and she gestured for Te'Kala to sit on some rocks near her. "You know our hearts are connected to our lakes, which nourish the woods and every other living thing in it?"

Te'Kala nodded.

"If our lakes are tainted then everything connected to it would be affected. Look around." Lasirena showed her a mucky, dark goo that stuck to the banks and muddled the water. Te'Kala scrunched up her nose and then looked at the sickly trees around them. They held nothing of the vivacity and healthy glow of Letheon's woods.

"I hadn't realized... Is your lake sick, Lasirena?"

The sprite nodded. "Water Sprites heartlessly douse fire demons and I believe that horrible act has now taken a toll on them. I, of course, have attempted to save other sprites by allowing them to fuse with my lake, but I fear some of their malice has begun tainting my own waters."

"That's terrible. Why did you never tell me?" Te'Kala leaned forward, frowning in concern.

"I didn't mean to trouble you, my love. You would have felt burdened to stay close to me at all times." Lasirena's water glided before Te'Kala in a caressing gesture before returning to the lake. "I believe that after the horrid sins Water Sprites have committed against your kind, our cold-hearted natures need a little warmth to keep this darkness, this illness, at bay and grant us strength."

"My fire is good for something?" Te'Kala asked, looking around the forest. She didn't seem to be helping much, though.

"You see, that's why I can't have anyone take you from me. You're far too precious. That male sprite must've feared what was to come to his lake and attempted to trick you to stay. He wouldn't care for you like I do."

Te'Kala scratched her cheek. "Letheon's lake didn't look sick, though. His woods were healthy and the water was pristine..."

"Did you not listen to a word I said?!" Lasirena's voice rung through the air. "I forbid you to see that male—" The sprite blinked and smoothed her hair back. Te'Kala hugged her knees to her chest as Lasirena smiled again. "Healthy, you say, beloved?"

Nodding was the only thing Te'Kala managed to do. She carefully watched as the sprite walked back to her lake, dipping a webbed toe in the water. Lasirena muttered under her breath, but Te'Kala didn't dare ask what she said.

"My love," Lasirena said, smiling sweetly. "We are friends, are we not? Our affection toward each other gives us power, does it not?"

"You are my friend, Lasirena," Te'Kala said, scratching her cheek once more. "Are you...feeling all right?"

"Yes, beloved, I think I feel very good." Murky goop floated on the surface of the water, slithering by Lasirena's feet, though the sprite hardly paid it any mind. "I have been helping other lakes for so long, it has taken a toll on my own health, as you can see. Perhaps your new friend could be of service. If he truly is as healthy as you claim he is, he could help me. He could fuse with my lake and perhaps that would cleanse it of this filth."

"Do you think that would work?" Te'Kala wanted to help her friend, but a ripple ran down her spine. She never questioned her friend about anything before, so why were things different this time? Was it the darkness in the lake that made Lasirena behave so strangely?

"Only if you're quick about it, my love." Lasirena twirled a finger around a lock of white hair. "Or do you not wish to help me, and rather watch me perish? Grant that male sprite all your powers?"

Te'Kala quickly stood. "Of course not—Letheon is not like that. I know he'll help, if I asked." She straightened. "I'll bring him here. I'll set off in the morning. Do you think you could hold on until then?"

A wide smile appeared on Lasirena's face. "Very well. Do be careful when you meet him. I don't like it when you leave me alone too long, but I trust in you. I know I can depend on you. I know you'd never leave me."

The edge in her voice stung Te'Kala, but her mind spun. As Lasirena continued babbling like a brook, Te'Kala tried to shake off the unease settling in her chest. There was a foulness to the air she couldn't put her finger on. Lasirena was adamant Letheon was up to something devious, but now wished for him to help her. Had the sickness affected Lasirena's mind already?

Te'Kala looked up at the pallid moon and wished she had offered to leave now. She wanted to see Letheon and hoped he really did know how to help.

Scorch marks trailed through the dirt of the forest floor as Te'Kala set off to Letheon's lake the next day. The moment she left Lasirena's lake behind her, Te'Kala felt like she could breathe again. She never felt that way, though she never usually strayed far enough to notice a difference. All night she wondered if her unease had anything to do with that.

For some reason, ever since she met Letheon, the world she'd known seemed so bleak. Letheon had brought color to her life in a way she had never experienced before. While Lasirena had always been kind to her and took her under her wing, it was different to how Letheon had treated her. Lasirena always managed to remind her of her fire's destructive powers. Letheon, however, made Te'Kala feel like she was more than just a fire demon who wreaked havoc.

A fire deity. You're not a demon, Te'Kala.

The sound of his voice and the image of his smiling face lingered in her mind. Why would Lasirena want her to stay away from him?

Shaking her head, Te'Kala continued her trek, determined to help Lasirena and simultaneously prove to her that Letheon had no ill intentions. *Maybe after he healed her, Lasirena would allow me to visit Letheon more often...*

The thought made Te'Kala hurry to his lake. The moment she set foot on his land, exhilaration swirled from her chest to her head and down to her toes. The lake and its surroundings welcomed her, and while the sensation brought a smile to her face, a jolt of nervousness ebbed through her.

Water Sprites were connected to their lakes. If Letheon had tried tricking her as Lasirena had said, that ill will would have shown in the plants, the trees, in the water. However, the lake was just as serene as she had left it. The breeze blew gently past her, the sun gleaming and glittering on the water's smooth surface. Critters drank from the lake, and though they acknowledged her presence, they did not run away. Luminescent dust escaped the delicate petals of flowers, the honeysuckle sweet in the fresh air. How could all of this light and peace be a facade?

Te'Kala walked to the banks of the small lake. The water was so clear she could see the bottom as though looking through glass. There wasn't any sign of darkness or putrefaction anywhere. Letheon was as healthy as could be.

What Te'Kala did find, was a bundle of dark red orbs, neatly gathered on the sand. She knelt down to touch one of them, and it caught fire immediately. The delicate aroma tickled her senses.

"You're back!"

Te'Kala jumped at the cheerful exclamation, shooting fireballs into Letheon's direction in a reflex. The Water Sprite ducked just in time as the fireballs sizzled and plunged into his lake.

He laughed when he resurfaced. "I'm starting to believe this is your way of saying hello," he said, holding up his hands in mock surrender.

Te'Kala tried to calm her breathing. "You shouldn't frighten me like that, I could have hit you!"

"Oh no, unexistence by doused rocks!" Letheon dramatically plunged himself into the water again before resurfacing, a lighthearted chuckle leaving his lips.

Despite her annoyance, Te'Kala cracked a smile. Lasirena's words of warning waned away. *How could someone who exudes so much warmth mean any harm?*

"I'm glad you came back," Letheon said, his voice much softer now, "I thought about you since you left. I was worried I would never see you again." His eyes glanced over her form. Te'Kala barely contained her flames from burning all over her body. She felt it sparking, the sensation soothing and frazzling at the same time.

"Why would you think I wouldn't visit you anymore?"

Letheon rubbed the back of his neck before sitting on the ground, a pink blush gracing his cheeks. "I thought I might have scared you away." He gestured between them. "Fire and water... Somehow the world decided we shouldn't be able to get along, and I guess I began to believe it."

Te'Kala sank down beside him, both of them facing the tranquil beauty of the lake. "Just because the world decided it, doesn't make it right. Didn't you say something like that yesterday?" Her ember eyes sparkled when Letheon grinned.

"Well, I'm happy you're here," he said.

"Did you miss me that much?" Te'Kala hid half her face behind her flaming hair when he nodded again. A pleasant silence fell between them, a kind of peace Te'Kala wished could go on for eternity. A flash of Lasirena's lake entered her mind, a stark contrast to the peacefulness she saw before her now.

"Letheon, if I were to tell you a friend of mine was ill and I knew you would be able to help, would you?"

Letheon's eyes widened slightly. "Did something happen? Is someone after you?"

Te'Kala frowned at his reaction. "No, she's sick and needs help.

Why would you ask if someone's after me?"

"*She*? O-oh, no reason." Rattled, Letheon attempted to mask his sudden nervousness behind a smile. "You're sure you're safe, there's no one hunting you? Because if there was, you'd be safe here. I can protect you, and your friend. You just have to bring her here as soon as you can. If she needs healing I can do that as well, just get her and I'll wait here—or better yet, I'll come with you. I can leave my lake for a while, it won't be a problem."

"Letheon, calm down," Te'Kala said, staring at him. "There's no one chasing me or my friend."

"Oh. Right." A sheepish grin graced his face as he rubbed the back of his head. He pursed his lips when Te'Kala continued watching him, waiting. "Are you going to ask?" he eventually said, unable to meet her gaze.

"Only if you feel comfortable telling me." Te'Kala pulled her knees to her chest, waiting for Letheon to reply. The Water Sprite narrowed his eyes for a moment.

"Yesterday, when I saw your fire near the shores of my lake, I briefly thought you were a friend I'd been waiting for."

Surprised by the answer, Te'Kala perked up. "A friend?"

Letheon slicked his green hair back and nodded. "It was a while back. Actually, he was a little bit like you, suspicious, jumpy, but very friendly. When he realized I had no intentions of putting out his flames, we became friends."

"That sounds familiar," Te'Kala said, burying her toes in the sand. "Why didn't you mention you had a fire deity friend before you met me?"

"You're not jealous, are you? I can assure you, you're much prettier than he was," Letheon said, eyes sparkling in mirth.

Hoping he wouldn't notice the bright flushes on her cheeks,

Te'Kala quickly focused on the conversation. "What happened to him?"

Letheon's shoulders slumped and the glint in his eyes faded. He dug his fingers in the sand. "I wish I knew. I keep waiting for him, but so far no luck. The last time I saw him he was supposed to come here with his lover. He said he ran into some trouble with someone who didn't agree with their union, I assume a Water Sprite. They were separated. Naturally I told him they'd be welcome here, and I offered to help him search for her, but he got distracted and needed to leave. He said he'd come back with her but he never did." As Letheon spoke, the leaves drooped, the wind laid down, until the entire forest stilled.

"Have you tried looking for him?" Te'Kala's voice was soft.

"Of course, I even asked other sprites, but they just laughed. I can't find him anywhere." Letheon didn't say more, casting his gaze away from her. She searched his face and recognized the sorrow in his deep blue eyes.

"I'm sure he's all right. Maybe he found his lover and they're together now." Te'Kala attempted to smile.

Letheon nodded and returned the gesture, but without conviction. "It's nice," he suddenly said, leaning back, "to see you so optimistic. Most fire deities are more reserved."

Te'Kala tucked a lock of hair behind her ear. "Is that bad?"

"Not at all." He chuckled. "I admire that optimism, though I take it you're careful when roaming the woods? There's something off about it lately, and if your friend is injured, I still think it would be best if you brought her here so I can help her and protect you."

"You would really protect me, even from one of your own?"

"Of course, I would—wow." Letheon appraised her. "You're glowing," he said, mesmerized. "Are you all right?"

Embarrassed, Te'Kala glanced away, looking at the sky instead.

"I'm fine," she said through clenched teeth.

"Are you sure?" Letheon moved closer, inspecting her face. From this proximity, she was astonished at how his eyes really did look like pools of deep blue water, except the thought of drowning in them didn't frighten her. Lasirena had been worried she'd leave her side. Was this why?

Thinking of her friend, Te'Kala forced herself to look away. "You'd help my friend then, if I asked you?"

"If you'd ask me, I'd do anything." The coy smile on Letheon's handsome face faded when he became more serious. "What exactly happened to your friend to have become ill? All I know is fire deities don't get sick unless water got to them. Do you need me to make some Fool's Gold?"

"I'm afraid Fool's Gold won't work, unless there's a lake full of it." Te'Kala grimaced.

"I see. Well, why don't you bring her here and I'll see what I can do."

"I don't think I can do that either," said Te'Kala, wincing a little at the confused look on his face. "You'd have to come with me and see for yourself. I fear her illness has begun to spread and if nothing can be done, she might perish and the woods along with her."

"Along with her? Hold on. Your friend is a Water Sprite?" A smile tugged at the corner of his lips.

"Yes, but there's something wrong with her lake. I suppose she's always acted a little strange, but it's worsened. I fear something bad might happen if she can't be helped." Te'Kala wiggled her toes further into the sand. She sensed his eyes on her, but couldn't bring herself to look at him.

"You make friends with Water Sprites, spent a day speaking to one, and now wish to save another," Letheon said. The shells framing his eyes glimmered in the daylight. "And you call me strange?"

The grin on his face made Te'Kala smile as well. "Does that mean you'll help?"

Letheon narrowed his eyes in thought for a moment, then waved his hand in the direction of his lake. A blue shine coated the water briefly, bubbles floating up in multitudes.

"My lake welcomes all, save for those with ill intentions. This little bit of magic strengthens that," he said, without Te'Kala having to ask. Then he got up and waited for Te'Kala to do the same. "Lead the way."

"When you said your friend was sick, how sick is she precisely?"

Te'Kala and Letheon had long left the warm, cozy woods near his lake, stepping deeper into a dark and twisted forest. Letheon walked as close to Te'Kala as possible without dousing her, glancing around them.

"What happened here? It's almost as if everything is tinged with... wrongness." Spheres of water appeared around Letheon, taking the shape of peculiar creatures which lived in the water. They circled him like majestic guardians. Briefly, Te'Kala wondered whether she would ever be able to create something like that with her flames. "Beautiful..."

Letheon's eyes shimmered warmly, a delicate blush dusting his features. "Beautiful, you say? I guess I should work more on my fierceness. Beautiful magic helps win over hearts, but isn't very helpful in danger, I imagine."

Flustered, Te'Kala abruptly shut her mouth as though it would take back the word that slipped from her lips. But when she saw him smirking again, she puffed her cheeks and turned away.

"Her lake is tainted with a strange, dark substance," she said instead, focusing on the task at hand. "The sooner she gets healed, the better it would be for the forest as well." Te'Kala casted a sideways glance at the fretful Water Sprite. "You're not frightened, are you?"

"Me, frightened?" Letheon scoffed, his cheeks turning a brighter shade of red. "Of course I'm not frightened. I-I'm just concerned about you. Doesn't anything here worry you?"

Te'Kala hid a smile. "Yes, it does. If Lasirena doesn't get well soon, I don't know what might happen to the forest." The trees thinned out before them, leading them to a wide, open clearing. "We're here." Te'Kala quickened her pace as they approached the vast lake, only to stop in her tracks at the sight before her. She took a shaky breath, hardly able to believe this was the same place she had left behind mere hours ago.

The tree roots and branches had blackened, the leaves pallid and brittle. The water of the lake, once pristine, was blotted by algae, black sludge covered the edges and bubbled like a living entity. Not a single sound passed through. Even the wind lay down and barely whispered through the blades of dried grass.

Te'Kala heard the flickering *whoosh* of her own hair, and for the first time in her existence she imagined what it would be like to feel cold. Beside her, Letheon looked around in shocked awe.

"You want me to heal *this*? You're an optimist, aren't you?"

Te'Kala glared at him and threw a small ball of fire at his head. On reflex, one of his guardians doused it, though the metallic lump went through the water and still hit its target. Letheon rubbed his head, wincing.

"There's more where that came from." Te'Kala crossed her arms as Letheon raised his hands.

"Noted." He gave her a little smirk and she quickly turned away, cheeks burning. Letheon looked around, kneeling down to touch the soil. Te'Kala watched him sniffing the earth before he moved to the water. A deep frown settled on his face.

"What did you say the name of your friend was?"

"Lasirena," Te'Kala said, standing beside him. "Is there something wrong?"

"Lasirena..." Letheon muttered under his breath, hovering his hand over the water. Barely had he touched it or he drew back, like something had come out snapping at his fingers. He turned around abruptly, startling Te'Kala. "We have to leave."

"What? But, her lake... I don't understand, I thought you said you would help me."

"Te'Kala, if this was any other Water Sprite I would, but it's dangerous here. Remember what I said about a foulness in this part of the woods? I couldn't put my finger on it then, but now I know why. It's the lake." Letheon reached for her before realizing the futility of it. "I don't know what Lasirena said to you, but a sprite's lake doesn't become like this without a reason. In fact, I wouldn't be surprised if she was the person my friend mentioned was chasing him and his lover."

"Her lake became this way because she helped other Water Sprites clean their lakes," Te'Kala said, taken aback by Letheon's sudden urgency and panic. "She said other sprites became ill because they extinguished fire deities for sport and because she helped them cleanse their water, some of that illness festered in her own lake."

Letheon blanched. "How did Lasirena claim to have helped these sprites?"

Te'Kala pursed her lips. "She fused her lake with theirs." Letheon's eyes widened at her words. "Is...that not how you heal each other?"

"Te'Kala, we should go. If she is as sick as you claim she is, we're not safe here."

"What do you mean? Lasirena would never hurt me."

"But there is a chance she's hurt others instead. Her own kind." Letheon gazed into her eyes. "Water Sprites are already connected with one another, that's how I could sense something wrong in this part of the forest. If she's been fusing with other Water Sprites, it's not to cleanse them."

Te'Kala frowned, stumbling to get the words out of her mouth with the lump in her throat. "What is it for then?"

Letheon fell silent a moment, grimacing. "Water Sprites do not fuse with one another because doing so would mean giving one's power and one's life to the sprite with more strength. I think Lasirena's lake is tainted, not because she healed sprites who doused fire deities, but because of her own greed. That sludge"—he pointed at the black slime at the edges—"is her own darkness eating away at her."

Te'Kala exhaled, shaking her head. "You're wrong. Lasirena would never do that, why would she, when she's already the guardian of the biggest lake in this forest?"

"I know it's difficult to hear, but you have to trust me, Te'Kala. I don't know why Lasirena told you a different story, but there's a malice in her waters. We should leave." Letheon had barely uttered the last words, when a tremble erupted from the lake.

Trying to keep her balance, Te'Kala dug her heels in the sand. The water bubbled, and slimy black tendrils slithered underneath, creeping toward the unsuspecting fire deity, reaching for her like gnarled hands. The trembling ceased, but before Te'Kala could move away from the lake, the tendrils shot forward with sharp, oozing claws.

Petrified, Te'Kala stared at the frightening sight of oblivion closing in on her. She would have been swallowed whole, had Letheon's shout not awoken her from shock.

"Move aside!"

A trident of water slashed through the sludge, whizzing past Te'Kala's face. A water creature with rows of sharp teeth swam forward and bit through the remaining darkness. The blackness dissipated and slunk back into the murky water.

"Are you all right?" Letheon stood beside her, examining her with his gaze. "I told you it's dangerous here!"

"What was that?" Te'Kala panted, gazing at the tendrils shrinking back into the murky water. Her flames flickered, covering her body like a cloak caught on fire.

"Are you injured, Te'Kala?" Letheon asked.

"I don't think so..." She shuddered, stepping away from the lake, glancing at the dark spots with renewed caution. "That's never happened before," she said, turning to Letheon. "Thank you."

"I told you I'd protect you." Letheon gestured for her to move further away from the lake. "Come with me, Te'Kala. We can't stay here."

"But, I can't leave Lasirena. The things she did— perhaps she was already sick. If that's the case, there must be something we can still do to save her."

"Te'Kala, I'm sorry, but there's no saving this. She might be gone already. Please, come with me." Letheon extended his hand. Te'Kala's hand hovered over his, knowing that she could never touch him. A knot tightened in her stomach.

Te'Kala moved toward him, opening her mouth to speak when black tendrils coiled from the waters once more, this time covering Letheon's limbs and forcefully throwing him sideways, away from

Te'Kala.

The fire deity gasped, watching as he slammed against a tree and fell down with a loud thud.

"Letheon!" Te'Kala went to check on him, but the loud rumble from the lake halted her steps. Something bubbled violently in the rippling water until waves formed, a maelstrom appearing in the center. Thick fog rose like steam, veiling the water. From within its murky depths, a figure emerged.

Te'Kala hardly recognized Lasirena. A blackness trailed behind her as she walked on water, though each step she took resounded with a sizzle, a nasty hiss Te'Kala couldn't quite place. When she looked the Water Sprite in the eye, a terrifying madness gleamed in her sea green eyes.

Lasirena's white hair floated behind her, delicate cracks forming on her creamy skin. Shards of ice rotated around her like deadly crystals.

Te'Kala jumped when those eyes looked straight at her.

"Beloved, I feared you left me..." A magical pressure built up from Lasirena and Te'Kala stepped back. The black tendrils slithered over the misty water, celebrating the Water Sprite's presence.

Was Letheon right? Were they already too late?

"Lasirena—" Te'Kala didn't know what to say. The Water Sprite's eyes flashed a sea green one moment and blazed a fierce red the next.

"Did he hurt you, beloved? That cruel thing?" The water trembled when Lasirena glared at Letheon, who was trying to get back on his feet. "Did he fill your head with pretty lies to steal you away from me?"

The tendrils coiled within the water, gliding against Lasirena like obedient pets. Te'Kala shuddered, fire engulfing her body.

"What happened to you, Lasirena? You weren't like this when I left this morning."

"Well, what was I to do and what was I to think when you were gone for such a long time, my love? For all I know, you could have deserted me for *that*." Lasirena glowered at Letheon.

"Why are you speaking like this? Letheon is here to help you."

"He is a filthy Water Sprite, beloved. They douse fire demons, they don't help!" Lasirena's voice was icy.

"Don't bother, Te'Kala. She's too far gone— she's tainted." Letheon groaned when he straightened, rolling his shoulders. Lasirena turned sharply toward him, her skin cracking further as if something fought its way from within to the surface.

"Tainted?" The black tendrils slid forward when Lasirena spoke. "How like a water worm to mistake absolute power for sickness!"

"Absolute pow— You corrupted your power with greed and misled Te'Kala," Letheon said, his voice deep and loud. "We are the guardians of this forest, but you've neglected your responsibility and duty in the vilest way possible!"

Te'Kala saw Lasirena glare at Letheon with so much hatred it struck fear into her heart. Was it still the sickness, or was this Lasirena's true nature?

"Did you fuse with other sprites to cure them, or to obtain their strength?" Te'Kala asked, balling her fists.

Lasirena glanced at her, a feigned smile on her face. "You would listen to the likes of him, beloved?"

"Did you heal them or strip them off of their powers and sent them to the Plane of Unexisting?" Te'Kala's flames flared.

A sneer appeared on the sprite's face when Te'Kala moved to stand before Letheon. "Tell me the truth."

Lasirena scoffed and breathed loudly through her nose. "Believe me when I say, everything I did was for us. For us to have power, for us to rule these woods together."

"What made you believe I want any of that?"

"Because it is what I want!"

The lake rumbled, the ground trembled, and the black tendrils writhed in delight.

Te'Kala was frozen, staring wide-eyed at Lasirena. "You lied to me. You played me for a fool! What else have you done?"

"More than you'll ever know. One day you'll understand why water worms like him must perish for us to live and be content." Lasirena pushed her hands forward and black tendrils shot over the land, heading straight for Letheon.

"Don't you dare harm him!" Te'Kala spread her arms, shielding Letheon from the attack.

"Te'Kala, don't. She doesn't want to hurt you. Escape while you can!" Letheon's plea fell on deaf ears.

"I won't let her harm you. You're not the only one capable of protecting someone they care about." Te'Kala's words seemed to sting Lasirena.

"Beloved, move aside. I'm giving you a chance at ultimate power and freedom, to rule together, side by side. He has nothing to offer you!"

There was no malice in Te'Kala's voice when she answered, "That's not what I want."

Lasirena stood still, her eyes boring into the fire deity. Spiky swirls of water and ice surrounded her. "I gave you everything. I give you a chance to be with me, and you refuse? You would choose *him*?!" A nearby tree creaked and groaned as the water of the lake boiled. The tree's bark burst open, black sludge oozing from the roots and pushing itself upward. It bubbled and spluttered, splashing against

Te'Kala's feet.

"Te'Kala!" Letheon rushed to her side.

"I'm all right," she said, feeling no pain. Both of them jolted back when the tree caught on fire.

Te'Kala narrowed her eyes. *Black magma?*

The air felt hot and cold at the same time. Dried blades of grass caught fire, yet the dirt was soaked with water. Te'Kala rushed back while Letheon created a moat of water around her to keep the sand she stood on dry. They looked at each other in silence, Letheon nodding at her.

Lasirena scowled. "You filthy water worm! I won't let you take Te'Kala away from me!"

Te'Kala summoned a wall of fire when icy shards shot toward them. "Stop this, Lasirena! Why are you like this? Letheon did nothing wrong! Unlike you, he is kind and good— a true protector. You've deceived me and murdered others, for what? Power?" Te'Kala's flames grew as she spoke of him, but she kept her gaze fixed on Lasirena. "I don't know you anymore, and I will not abide you hurting Letheon."

"You reject me?" Lasirena's mouth twisted, the cracks on her skin fanning out. Her arms trembled as she clenched her fists.

Te'Kala stepped away from her to stand closer to Letheon. His water guardians encircled them both.

Lasirena's lip quivered. "Beloved..." Silence fell when she stared at Te'Kala and Letheon, her sea green eyes narrowing before they flared red.

"So, you've made your choice..." The water underneath Lasirena swirled wildly. Fire covered the surface, the black magma creeping forward to cover the land. "Fine. If you wish to be with him, so be it!" With a deafening shriek, a tidal wave rose with a gesture of her hands, rushing relentlessly toward Te'Kala.

Letheon's scream ripped through the air. "Te'Kala, no!"

The water thundered like galloping horses, looming over her like a dome of impending doom. She made no attempt to protect herself, her flames already wavering. Glancing one last time at Letheon, she closed her eyes, waiting for the nothing to claim her.

Cold. Wet. Sensations she never thought she would've been able to feel without screaming in agony. Yet Te'Kala let the feelings flow through her body, rippling her skin painlessly.

Was this the Plane of Unexisting? How could she still *be* if she was sent into unexisting? If she was still *here*, would that mean...

"Letheon?"

Te'Kala looked around, hoping to see the Water Sprite, but instead she was surrounded by nothingness. A vast emptiness where she stared into an abyss and the hollow stared back. Even with her wispy flames burning, she saw nothing.

Was this what it was like to unexist? To be awake, surrounded by nothingness—worse, by loneliness? That couldn't be right. Surely if she was still here after being doused, there must be *something*!

Te'Kala looked at her hands, how normal they appeared. When she moved them, they were solid. Maybe she wasn't in the Plane of Unexisting, maybe Lasirena's water never doused her— she covered her ears when the rush of water echoed around her.

This couldn't be it. Was she doomed to roam here, never to see Letheon again?

The thought of his handsome face sent her heart racing. The joy welling up in her chest was swiftly doused when she realized she would never see him again, she would never hear him laugh or be able to speak to him anymore. She held on to the memory of him smiling at her, his green hair shining in the soft glow of the sun, deep blue eyes framed by glimmering, opalescent shells. A sob escaped her lips when she saw his mouth curl up in a cheeky grin.

Te'Kala gasped when bright diamond drops fell, lighting up in the abyss. She blinked in confusion when the drops floated back up, hovering near her. Te'Kala reached out and the drops moved and jiggled like liquid. Confused, Te'Kala touched her face and startled to find it wet. The diamond drops fell freely from her eyes.

"Am I—Are these..." She wiped her cheek, the drops glistening on her uninjured hand. "Tears?"

The drops brightened, glowing stronger than Te'Kala's flames, up to the point she was forced to shut her eyes against the light. The darkness waned and when Te'Kala regained her vision, the nothing was gone.

She looked around with wide eyes at a familiar forest, the scent of honeysuckle drifting in the gentle breeze, fresh blades of grass tickling her feet. The sensation was so new, laughter bubbled from her throat and for the first time ever, she dared touch the trees and the colorful flowers, in awe how they remained intact. Her flames didn't burn, they didn't destroy. Overcome by excitement, Te'Kala ran toward the glassy lake, dipping her toe in the water, marveling at how water felt against her skin.

"Letheon! You have to come see this, look, I don't feel any pa—"

A lump settled in her throat as she looked at the stillness of the forest. She moved away from the lake and sat down near the shore, pulling her knees up to her chest. Of course Letheon wasn't here. These woods and the lake before her might look like they were his lands, but whatever this place was, it couldn't be real.

Sighing, Te'Kala leaned her head against her knees, wondering why it still hurt to cry, even though her tears didn't burn her.

A sudden splash jolted her upright, her gaze drawn to the lake. The water rippled and waved as a form moved through them, as elegant as the sea creatures residing within it.

Could it be?

Te'Kala dared not rekindle that flame of hope, but her heart betrayed her. She rose when a figure broke through the surface, sweeping his green hair back and waving cheerfully at her. Tears blurred her vision, but she waved back eagerly, stumbling to meet him.

"Letheon!" Her voice broke with emotion, but she called his name again, walking into the water, ankle-deep, until she stopped. Why wasn't he rushing to meet her?

"Letheon? Letheon, it's me!" She caught her breath a moment. "I thought I would never see you again." The smile on her face faltered as Letheon continued walking, stopping a few feet away from her. Te'Kala felt like she could reach out and touch him, but he looked so distant.

"W-what's wrong?"

"I thought you'd forgotten about me," Letheon said, chuckling softly.

Te'Kala frowned. "What? Of course not, I could never forget about you, I l—" Te'Kala gasped when Letheon moved forward and continued walking—straight through her.

She turned to follow his movement as her breath hitched. She stopped cold when she saw Letheon walking to meet someone on shore, someone whose skin was red and orange like a fiery sunrise.

Te'Kala narrowed her eyes when she saw the male fire deity

greet Letheon with a wave of his own, but his movements weren't as smooth as Letheon's. His burning hair, light blue near the roots, was flickering and he fidgeted as he paced around the shore in small circles.

"What is..." Te'Kala followed. This version of Letheon could not see her, and the other fire deity showed no signs he'd noticed her either. She wasn't sure what was going on, but now she needed to know.

"Calm down, Te'Viro, I can't understand when you're raging on like that." Letheon's soothing voice seemed to have some effect on the fire deity. The male—Te'Viro—took a deep breath and calmed his movements.

"I'm sorry, you're right, I just—I don't know what to do."

"Starting at the beginning usually works," said Letheon, gesturing for Te'Viro to sit down on the sand as he did the same. "The last time we spoke you told me you were going to bring your lover here in order to escape someone's wrath. I'd expected you to arrive the same day, but that was well over a fortnight ago."

"That was my intention, to bring her here with me so we'd be safe, but..." Te'Viro swallowed as if it was difficult for him to breathe. "We were cursed, Letheon. I don't know precisely what happened, but as soon as it happened, she was gone! One moment we were standing next to each other, then a mist enveloped me and we were separated. I tried looking for her, but I couldn't find my way, the woods changed or something, I don't—" The fire deity sunk to the ground, his fingers tangled in his flaming hair.

Te'Kala watched silently, sitting next to Letheon. For a moment she was tempted to try and touch him, but Te'Viro jumping to his feet made her stumble back.

"I don't know what to do, Letheon," the fire deity said. "I have to find her before anything bad happens, but I've looked everywhere already."

Letheon hummed, scratching his chin. "I could go around and ask some of the Water Sprites. Maybe they've seen her—oh, um..." He scratched the back of his head, grimacing when Te'Viro looked horrified. "I'm sure they wouldn't douse her! She probably knows better than to walk toward lakes, right? Don't worry, I'll help you." He smiled widely but a look of unease settled on Te'Viro's face. He dug his feet deeper in the sand.

"Letheon, I should probably tell you..."

Te'Kala waited for Te'Viro to finish his sentence, but Letheon spoke over him.

"I'll ask around and help you search. Let me ask near the lakes, you do best to stay away from them—just to be safe. I heard from some F'Airies that one particular sprite has a tendency to act before asking questions. Her lake is supposed to be bigger than mine, but I can't remember her name though." He scratched his head. "The Earth Fays were complaining about her, said there was something off about the lands near her lake."

Te'Viro rushed forward, though he made sure not to touch Letheon. Te'Kala frowned at seeing him so excited. Why was she being shown this interaction in the first place?

"A bigger lake? Where is this lake?" Te'Viro asked, impatience ringing through his voice.

Letheon raised an eyebrow. "A few miles in that direction, you'll see when you have to turn back around since the woods feel different." He got up and shook the sand off of his body. "Best to avoid it—where are you going?" Letheon walked after Te'Viro when the fire deity moved away. "I just told you, you shouldn't go that way, haven't you been listening?"

"I heard you, and I know. I just…" Te'Viro took a deep breath, opening and closing his mouth. "You just made me think of something, that's all. I might have an idea where she could be, thank you. I promise I'll be back with her as soon as possible," he said, a weak smile tugging at the corner of his mouth. "You promise we'd still be welcome in your little sanctuary, right?"

Blinking and scratching his cheek, Letheon nodded. "Of course, as long as you don't have any ill intentions, and I'd happily welcome your lover as well, but…" He frowned at Te'Viro. "Is everything all right? I feel like you're not telling me something. You're not heading to that lake, are you?"

"I promise everything will make sense when we get back, Letheon." Te'Viro smiled. "I can't waste any more time, but I'll return. Thank you, my friend." With that, he hastily turned around and ran before Letheon had a chance to stop him.

Te'Kala saw his flames move through the forest and glanced at a worried Letheon. She reached out to touch a lock of his hair, but he didn't respond. "I'll be back soon, too," she whispered and ran after Te'Viro.

It didn't take long before the atmosphere of the woods changed, growing heavy and dark. Soon enough, Te'Kala stood near the shore of another lake she knew very well, her blood rushing through her ears when she saw Te'Viro boldly calling out to Lasirena.

Is he mad? No wonder he never returned to Letheon with his lover. His recklessness must've doused him.

Wait… She paused. *How does he know this is Lasirena's lake?*

"Lasirena! Where are you?" Te'Viro stood dangerously close to the water's edge. "Lasirena!"

Te'Kala moved forward when the sound of broken twigs caught her attention. She had half a mind to warn him, except she knew he wouldn't be able to hear her.

A wave of relief washed over her when another fire deity appeared from the woods. She was fierce, with long flaming hair that grew past her ankles, fire sparking at her fingertips. This must be Te'Viro's lover.

"Quickly, take her with you and head back to Letheon, you fool," Te'Kala said under her breath, but was surprised when Te'Viro staggered away from the female fire deity. Fire covered his body and burned like the sun when he faced her.

"Te'Irena." A guttural growl rumbled from his chest as he kept his distance. Bursts of fire encircled his body.

"My love. I'm impressed you found me." Unlike Te'Viro, this Te'Irena purred, her voice enticing like a dancing flame, with a certain burn intended to cause pain. Why was that familiar?

"I guess this means I still need to perfect my skills. It's not easy to conjure curses, you know." Te'Irena smiled but Te'Kala shivered at the ease of her confession. What was going on here? A fire deity cursing another fire deity? That made no sense!

"Where is she? Where is Lasirena?" Te'Viro moved back when Te'Irena stepped forward, never taking his eyes off of her.

"Do you not understand how curses work, my love?" She sighed. "I wish you could see that I am doing this for you—for us. It's an abomination, unnatural, vile—"

"It's love. Though I'm hardly surprised love would appear foul to someone who only knows resentment and hatred in their heart."

Te'Irena sneered while Te'Kala continued watching in confusion. *What is he talking about?*

"You think she won't destroy you? Fire and water do not mix, Te'Viro!" Te'Irena's voice bellowed through the forest and still rang in Te'Kala's ears. Her heart beat so loudly, she thought it'd explode.

"That is not up to you to decide! If we are capable to love each other, there's no reason for any of us to live in fear of one another." Te'Viro circled Te'Irena as she moved, making sure he could keep her in sight.

"You would so easily forget how many of our kind she has murdered?" Flames danced over Te'Irena's skin, her eyes glowing.

"She didn't know any better! She learned!"

"You think she truly loves you? Te'Viro, you're smarter than that," said Te'Irena, standing near the shore. "She loves power. The biggest lake in these woods is under her rule, and with a fearsome fire demon by her side, she'd become unstoppable. Is that what you truly want? For her to douse more of our kind as she sees fit, to use you to burn all others who would dare oppose her?"

Te'Viro clacked his tongue, shaking his head. "That's not true and you know it. It's you who desires power, you who have become twisted and tinged with darkness." He widened his stance and straightened. "You cannot separate us, Te'Irena. We strive to make this world a safer and peaceful place for all. That still includes you. There's no reason for you to turn away from the light."

Te'Kala had watched the interaction with bated breath, a knot still lodged in her throat. The longer she looked at Te'Irena, the more the uneasy feeling swirled in her stomach.

"What will it take for you to see? That you and her are an abomination that can never be?"

Te'Viro sighed at Te'Irena's bitterness and shook his head. "One day I hope you'll understand. I can overcome anything with her. We will make this world better, make it more welcoming."

Te'Irena's jaw locked, the fire over her body flowing erratically. "We could have made the world ours, you and I. Show everyone fire is not to be tamed, but respected. We could be the true, rightful rulers of these woods." She inhaled deeply. "Yet you choose her over me?"

Te'Kala gasped, recognizing the gleam in Te'Irena's eyes, the rush of water thundering in her ears. When black tendrils grew from Te'Irena's long hair and slithered over the earth, Te'Kala finally understood the meaning of blood running cold in her veins.

"Love is strange, Te'Irena. I fear it." Te'Viro's voice trembled. "I fear its strength, I fear how weak it makes me feel. I wish I could cure myself of it, but at the same time I can't imagine existing without it—" He swallowed when he looked at her. His eyes gleamed with emotion. "Even if I had a choice, I'd still choose her."

The ground shook briefly, causing Te'Kala to lean against a rock to keep her balance.

"Infected. You're infected..." Te'Irena snapped her fingers and a low rumble erupted from the lake. "Very well. I kept you apart for your own good, Te'Viro, but you desire so desperately to be together? Very well." With a wave of her hand, a figure emerged from the water, bound in the black tendrils that grew from Te'Irena's hair.

Te'Kala's eyes widened when she recognized Lasirena, gasping for breath, crying.

"Lasirena!" Te'Viro nearly jumped into the lake but turned to Te'Irena instead. "Release her!"

"No! Te'Viro, please, run! Stay away!" The Water Sprite coughed, her voice fragile. "Please, leave." The pain on her face stunned him.

"I can't leave you."

A small smile appeared on Lasirena's face but she still shook her head. "Please, I can't—Te'Viro, she—" Black tendrils crept over Lasirena's mouth, muffling her cries.

"Why are you doing this?!" Te'Viro balled his fists when he looked at Te'Irena. His flames grew.

"I'm not doing anything, my love. You did this to yourself," she said, her voice carrying through the wind, a sickening smog flowing from the tendrils. Her eyes glowed and her fire fused with the smoke, the air becoming thick with a foul kind of magic that made Te'Kala gag.

"Be with each other. Go," Te'Irena suddenly said, the black tendrils slipping away from Lasirena's struggling form. "Let your love for each other consume you, let desire to become as one overwhelm you." Her voice echoed through the forest, the grass bending away from them, the leaves rustling so loudly like they meant to escape the branches that carried them.

"What are you doing?" Te'Viro inhaled sharply, his fire diminishing with each breath he took. "Te'Irena, what have you done?"

"If you can't be cured by your infection, then I will spare you the suffering." She turned towards Lasirena, who tried her best to remain on her lake, but the curse Te'Irena uttered was so foul, so strong, she never stood a chance. "Show me how much you claim to love him."

"Te'Irena, please, don't! Tell us to never be together again and we'll stay apart, but please, don't force me to do this!" Lasirena tried kneeling, but the water moved her to the shore, to Te'Viro who had sunk to his knees, unable to move, unable to run.

"I'm giving you what you want, to be together, forever as one."

Te'Kala had never seen eyes so cold before. She would have shuddered seeing it on anyone's face, but on a fire deity... She understood why some would refer to them as *demons*.

"Lasirena, it's all right," Te'Viro said, drawing deep breaths. "We tried." A faint smile appeared on his face as Lasirena attempted to beam back through her tears.

"I love you," she whispered, the ground shifting, moving her closer to Te'Viro even though she hardly moved herself.

Te'Irena sneered. "Show him what that love does to him!"

Te'Viro stood to meet Lasirena, the smile still on his face, gazing at her as if she was the only thing he could see. "It's all right," he said to her, the black mist pushing them closer to each other. Te'Kala could barely watch them. She stood stiff with tension, unable to do anything.

Lasirena wept when Te'Viro touched her face through the pain he must've felt and tilted her head back to kiss her. As their kiss deepened, a sickening sizzle accompanied their last words to one another. Te'Viro's fire slowly doused, but he never cried out, drowning into Lasirena's embrace as her water consumed him. A final spark jolted from his chest, jumping toward her heart before that doused as well.

The Water Sprite sunk to her knees and wailed loudly, the sound so heart-wrenching, Te'Kala felt teardrops fall from her eyes again.

With the horrid deed done, Te'Irena stepped forward, looming over Lasirena. Without warning, the fire *demon* roughly grabbed the Water Sprite's face, her hand hissing, but her flames still burning. The black tendrils spread to the lake, black smog lingering in the air. "My, my, my... Such destructive power you Water Sprites yield."

Lasirena tried to move away from Te'Irena, but the fire demon tightened her grip. "This was the result of your love. Was it worth it?"

"You did this!" Lasirena said, gasping for breath. "You killed him!"

"Well, I thought your so-called love could overcome everything, but I suppose I was wrong." Te'Irena covered her mouth with her free hand. "Oops."

"You're heartless!" Lasirena shrieked, the water in the lake responding to her anger as it rushed toward the fire demon, but Te'Irena simply conjured a wall of scorching flame the water could not penetrate, strengthened by the black tendrils. "You will never find the happiness you long for!"

"Te'Viro might have taken that happiness away when he chose you, but I can hardly blame him for being attracted by so much power." A glaze of empty madness shaded Te'Irena's eyes. She grabbed Lasirena's neck, moved closer to the struggling Water Sprite. "Dry those tears, beloved. If your power is such a pain to you, allow me to relieve you of that burden."

Te'Kala covered her ears when Lasirena started screaming, her voice muffled when Te'Irena kissed her—drank her. They disintegrated and integrated into one another, fire and water battling in the struggle to become the victor, but Te'Kala knew who would win. She saw Te'Irena reborn, looking at her new appearance. She wriggled her fingers and ran them through her silky hair. Her fiery eyes changed into a sea green before they snapped to Te'Kala, who jolted at the sudden acknowledgment.

The black tendrils flew forward and as she turned to run, she froze in her steps. Te'Viro and the real Lasirena stood before Te'Kala, holding hands, watching her as the forest crumbled away to nothingness once more. The sudden silence unnerved Te'Kala, but she kept looking at Te'Viro and Lasirena, not knowing what to say.

Te'Kala twitched when both of them held out their hands and touched either side of her shoulders. She still expected to sizzle when Lasirena touched her, but once again, she felt no pain.

Emotions ebbed and flowed through her, feelings of fragile love and profound happiness, of bitter loss and sorrowful regret. But through all of this, she felt another sensation simmering in the background—hope.

"I wish I could have helped you," she said, thinking about Letheon. What would Te'Irena do to him?

"I can't go back, can I?" Desperation clung to her heart at the thought of Letheon in danger. "Is there a way for me to warn him? You must've shown me all of this for a reason, please—" Te'Kala fell quiet when neither Te'Viro nor Lasirena seemed to want to answer her.

She sighed. "Te'Irena won't stop, will she?" Te'Kala ran her fingers through her hair, imagining Letheon's smile, his comforting laugh. This couldn't be it. How could Te'Irena's darkness win like this?

As Te'Kala racked her brain, Te'Viro and Lasirena gazed at each other with loving smiles before they reached to Te'Kala once more. The fire deity blinked at Te'Viro's scorching touch and winced at how cool Lasirena's hand felt against her shoulder. They closed their eyes as memories of Letheon flooded Te'Kala's mind. The images flashed as heat and cold soared through her body, making her writhe, but it all stopped when she saw Letheon before her, clear as day, leaning his head against hers before planting a chaste kiss on her lips. A brightness pushed away the darkness, and a searing pain enveloped her senses, until everything faded out.

Darkness was everywhere. Even when she tried to move, Te'Kala felt imprisoned by stone. Was this it? Was she finally fading into unexistence?

Te'Kala groaned, tried to move, tried to see something. The pitch blackness around her was crushing.

A blue glow sprung into being, catching her eye. She gasped when a fiery orange glow followed. They mixed together, oscillating, a pleasant heat warming her body and a soothing coolness awakening a dormant spark inside her.

She took a deep, invigorating breath as her stone prison began to crumble. *Where am I?*

A pleasant shiver ran through her hand, as if someone held it. It was only now Te'Kala realized she could hear voices coming from outside her prison.

"You've taken everything from me." *Lasirena? No. Te'Irena.*

"Then we are even. Where did your hatred come from, Lasirena? Dousing fire deities for sport, killing lovers for wanting to be together—when have you grown so bitter?"

Te'Kala's heart fluttered when she recognized Letheon's voice, only to be replaced by panic. *He doesn't know. I have to warn him!*

"You know nothing of my pain!" Te'Irena said. "But you will, soon."

"What will you do? You've already taken Te'Kala from me! You're going to try and drown a Water Sprite?"

"My dear, you have no idea what I can do!"

Te'Kala heard Letheon gasp and a flaming fury rose from her chest. An unfamiliar power surged through her and the stone holding her in place ruptured. As the rock split, a deep orange glow with splotches of blue burst through and searing hot light flaked the remaining crust away. When she opened her fiery eyes she saw Te'Irena in the guise of Lasirena before her, her skin cracked and barely able to contain her true nature. Beside Te'Kala stood Letheon, gaping at her, blinking rapidly as if he didn't believe his eyes.

The thundering of water rushing toward her entered her mind once more, but Te'Kala was less fearful this time. She remembered Te'Irena had doused her, that she should be in the Plane of Unexisting, but perhaps Te'Viro and the real Lasirena had helped her after all. Te'Kala looked over her transformation in curious bewilderment, her glowing skin splotched with a deep iridescent blue. When she touched her hair she noticed streaks of ash flowed through her flaming hair, and bangles of lava circulated her arms and ankles.

"How—"

Te'Kala's gaze snapped to Te'Irena, who shook her head. "No! You can't be—! You think this changes anything? I've destroyed you once and I will do so again, you horrid mutant, you foul—"

Before she could even scream, a stream of lava flung her back, dunking her into the boiling lake with a loud splash. Blue and orange flames covered Te'Kala as she shot another stream of lava after Te'Irena for good measure. Then, she turned to Letheon, smiling at him, relieved he wasn't hurt.

Letheon stared at her, unmoving, though his dark blue eyes shone with emotion.

Te'Kala formed a small ball of fire and chucked it at him. The sprite jolted and doused it deftly, catching the rock with a crooked grin on his face. "You're really here?" The grin spread. "But, how—" He watched as Te'Kala took his hand without wincing, a pure glimmer of light appearing between their hands. He gasped softly when he saw his own hand had turned a soft orange.

"Fear and hatred can be overcome by a special spark," Te'Kala whispered, closing the gap between them. "You were right, Letheon. There was a malice in her waters but it wasn't Lasirena. She would never have asked other Sprites to fuse with her. She would never have doused fire deities for sport or desire their power."

Letheon lifted an eyebrow. "Do you not remember who doused you just now?"

Te'Kala shook her head. "That was Te'Irena, a fire demon. She murdered Lasirena and somehow fused with her and took her place."

"What? How—Why would she do that?"

"Because Lasirena fell in love with Te'Viro, your friend, and he loved her. Te'Irena thought their union to be an abomination. She couldn't stomach the idea of Te'Viro leaving her for a Water Sprite who had doused fire deities before. In her bitterness, madness and darkness grew inside her and she cursed them, used their love for each other against them."

Letheon swallowed, clenching his fingers over Te'Kala's hand. "How did she get that kind of power?"

Te'Kala motioned to the black ooze drifting in the lake, and the tendrils on the ground. "If love can be turned into a strength, I think hatred can too."

"Then we have to go, come." Letheon pulled Te'Kala along, but the fire deity held him back.

"And leave the lake that nourishes the bigger part of the forest like this? What of Te'Irena? Do we leave her to exist and hurt others?"

Sighing, Letheon locked his jaw before looking around. He ran his free hand through his hair and nodded. "I don't know what we can do about Te'Irena, but perhaps I can do this." He ran to the lake. Doing his best to avoid the murky goop, water swirled around him, glowing brightly. He moved his hands as the water around his feet began to clear. The water flowed at his command before it plunged into the murky lake. A bright blue light shone, dispelling the black tendrils and purifying the lake as best as possible. While Letheon cleaned the water, the forest gained more color, a breath of life sweeping over the broken trees and burned earth—healing, but never mending.

"I don't think I can clean the madness Te'Irena tainted it with, but the woods won't have to suffer because of her this way. They can live."

"Will it work?"

"I hope so."

Letheon reached out to take Te'Kala's hand again when a sudden tremble broke them apart, the lake boiling and rippling. A burst of water shot out from the center of the lake and evaporated, a seething Te'Irena emerging from its depth.

"What did you do?!" Her shriek caused the couple to step back, the sound of it almost as horrid as her new appearance. Her skin flaked away to reveal a matted orange underneath, blackened when touched by water. Her eyes gleamed a fiery ember and part of her face broke open to reveal the fire demon inside. Her white hair flowed with sparks of flames that could not fully ignite, the other half of her face translucent and pale, black veins trailing under the skin. She shot a jet of scalding water at the couple, but Te'Kala rushed forward. Flames blazed around her body, the heat so scorching, Letheon was forced to step back.

Te'Irena's water evaporated with a sizzle and even when she ceased her attack, Te'Kala still burned, walking steadily toward her.

"Burn all you want, I doused you once I can do so again and I'll force you to take that water worm with you!" Te'Irena's words were weakened by her wavering eyes as Te'Kala's flames were so hot, the water of the lake began to disperse.

"Enough, Te'Irena. You've caused enough pain." Te'Kala's plea fell on deaf ears. The raging fire demon used the remaining black tendrils to attack.

Te'Kala's flames singed the blackness with ease as panic set in Te'Irena's face.

"You think a little spark of love makes you powerful? I hold fire and water under my command!"

"Yes"—Te'Kala advanced, the water evaporating where she drew near—"it's true I know very little of love, but I know it fills me with more strength than your darkness ever could."

Te'Irena laughed. "You sound just like Te'Viro. Look where his love brought him!"

"How do you think I came back?" Te'Kala moved closer, hesitation shining in Te'Irena's eyes. "Te'Viro and Lasirena are together, and they brought me back to Letheon."

Te'Irena bristled, her breathing erratic. "You lie! I separated them forever!"

"Your curse is not that strong," Te'Kala said, her flames burning hotter as the vapor thickened the air.

"Not strong?" Te'Irena hissed in pain as the water in the lake continued to disperse. "Even without the water in this lake, I can still send you to unexistence!" Te'Irena shrieked when Te'Kala's flames boiled the water slowly, the black tendrils disintegrating and wailing in anguish.

"In your blind pursuit of revenge and power you fused yourself with Lasirena and other Water Sprites..."

"Which makes me more powerful than you'll ever be!" Te'Irena's skin cracked and boiled at the same time. The black tendrils jolted and covered her feet, rendering her motionless.

"Which means your life is tied to this lake as well. If the lake of a Water Sprite dries up, the woods nourished by the water will wither along with them. Without this lake you will perish, too." There was no grudge in Te'Kala's voice as Te'Irena's eyes widened and her face contorted in pain. The water boiled away, steaming, and Te'Irena's skin paled, her fire waning. Letting out an anguished gasp, she buckled over, the black tendrils slithering around her.

"You've caused so much pain. The world would be better without the likes of you in it..." Te'Kala's fire grew.

Te'Irena shrunk back. "Stop," she moaned, her voice but a whisper. "Stop!"

"Te'Kala!" Letheon's voice rang over the ruckus. Te'Kala's flames simmered down in an instant. She turned to look at him.

"If she is sent to a state of unexisting, the lake will die. These woods do not deserve that," Letheon said, extending his hand to her. "And you are better than her."

Te'Kala moved back to the shore to hold his hand, though the frown hadn't left her face. "What she did to Te'Viro and Lasirena—"

"Is done." A look of pity flashed across his face before he hardened his expression toward Te'Irena. "You thought you separated them, but their love persevered and brought Te'Kala back to me. You wanted the power of a Water Sprite, and now your fate is tied to this lake. Your anger and madness are your own, Te'Irena, you can never harm us anymore."

Te'Kala gazed at Letheon and drew closer. He looked back at her, intertwining his fingers with hers.

"Curse you!" Te'Irena's voice broke, but her fire could not rage as it had before. The water barely responded to the venom in her words, until she touched the black tendrils. "Unable to harm you, you say? You couldn't heal this lake, my powers are seeping into the ground as we speak! I will not be made weaker by abominations like you!"

With the last bit of magic she possessed, Te'Irena gripped the black tendrils. They began to glow green, burrowing themselves deep in the ground. "A curse upon you and all those mad enough to fall in love with those they are meant to hate! May their desire cause them torment, may their love hurt and ruin them, turn them into the monsters they are, drive them apart!"

A blast of wind nearly knocked them over. A thick mist approached from the lake.

"Letheon!" Te'Kala grabbed him tight as the mist enveloped him, but her hands were lost in the fog as he began to vanish. "Letheon, no! Hold on to me!" She reached for him but the Water Sprite shook his head.

"Te'Kala, it'll be okay!" he said, struggling as the mist thickened around him. "I know you'll find me, there's one place she can't touch!"

"Letheon, no!" She swung her arms around him, but grabbed a fist full of air instead. He'd vanished.

Trembling, Te'Kala sharply turned to confront Te'Irena—only to find she had disappeared as well. The black tendrils pulsated with a glowing green light and when she burned them, they glowed brighter but remained rooted in the land.

She ran her hands over her face, slicking her hair back. "One place she can't touch, one place she can't touch..." Te'Kala paced in circles, unsure whether the creeping feeling of frustrating madness was due to the curse or concern for Letheon's safety. *Letheon...*

Te'Kala groaned and smacked her forehead. "Of course!" Without wasting any more time, Te'Kala ran through the forest, barely taking note of trees that began to move on their own volition, their roots attempting to get in her way. But Te'Kala knew which way to go, she could never get lost to find Letheon's lake. All were welcome there, save for those with ill intentions.

However, Te'Kala's hope sank into her stomach when she arrived at his lake to see a large egg-shaped dome in its place. She ran around it, searching for an entrance, but the edifice was made out of thick vines and strong roots, wild flowers growing to cover each crook and cranny.

"No," she said, touching the plants in hopes her flames would destroy them. "Open!" Te'Kala cried out as loudly as she could, especially when the plants remained intact, no matter how hot her fire burned.

"Te'Kala?"

"Letheon?" The fire deity placed her ear against the plants, then tried to peer through the thick foliage.

"Te'Kala! I knew Te'Irena wouldn't be able to separate us."

His lighthearted chuckle brought a smile to her face. "Did you not notice the gigantic dome keeping us apart?"

"Oh, this? Well, I've wanted to redecorate for some time now."

Te'Kala didn't know how Letheon managed to joke around, but a weak chuckle left her throat anyway. "It covered your entire lake."

"And then some," Letheon said, a short silence falling between them. "I think her curse is working a little. I think I'm going mad without you."

"This can't be it, Letheon. After everything, she wins? How are we supposed to break a curse like this?"

"We can't, but that's what she's hoping for, that we'll be broken by this. She hopes the one power she can never have will be the one that destroys us. If we allow that to happen, that's when she wins."

"Then what can we do?" Te'Kala wasn't sure whether Letheon heard her, her voice was so quiet.

"Have you tried burning it?" he asked.

"I'm touching it right now and it won't catch fire." She let the flames dance over her hand, letting it burn freely to no effect. "Will we never see each other again?"

"We can't break this spell, but perhaps..." When Letheon didn't finish his sentence, Te'Kala tried peering through the plants once more.

"Letheon? What is it? Are you still there?" Te'Kala stepped back when the edifice trembled.

"Stand back, Te'Kala!" His shout was quickly followed by a deafening rush of water, crashing against the sturdy foliage of the dome. They remained unrelenting.

"What are you doing? It's not working, Letheon, please, stop, you'll exhaust yourself."

"No, I won't stop and I won't give in! If we can't break this blasted wall and we can't lift her curse, then I'll expand it!" The rush of water became louder and Te'Kala saw the dome react. The vines and moss grew more dense, but then they moved, crawling down to the earth, a sheen of blue magic covering them. They extended into the forest and Te'Kala carefully stepped aside when some of them even turned into freshly sprung brooks. Like veins they cut through the green lands, leaving a trail of new flowers, reeds and rushes near its banks. They whistled melodically when the wind blew through them.

Letheon grunted from the inside. "This is my lake! It feeds this part of the woods, and Te'Irena is not the only one with magic. Yes, her curse will persevere, but despite the heartache she has caused, those Infected Lovers affected by her cruelty will find solace here. Those with love in their hearts will always be able to find each other, safely harbored from those who resent them!"

The moment Letheon muttered the words, a rift appeared in the edifice before Te'Kala and as the opening widened, she was greeted by a tired Letheon. Panting, and wiping the sweat from his brow, he grinned as she ran to meet him.

"How did you do that?" she asked, easily embracing him. A gentle sizzle sounded when they touched, but neither felt any pain.

"Have you forgotten my lake contains something special?"

"What, you?"

"Correct." Letheon rubbed his nose against hers. "And you. Let's see Te'Irena do something now."

Te'Kala pulled away from him. "What if she finds us?"

"She won't. This place is made for lovers, not wretched souls like her."

Te'Kala nodded slowly, gazing at the paradise within the dome, a welcoming sanctuary nourished and protected by Letheon's lake. Then, his words sunk in and blushes crept over her cheeks. "So... We are lovers, then?"

Letheon sighed before beaming another grin. "Afraid so."

"A fire deity and Water Sprite in love. Sounds absolutely crazy," Te'Kala said with a smile of her own.

Letheon pulled her toward him and kissed her forehead. "That's how you know it's real."

While Te'Kala and Letheon accepted their fate of never being able to leave the sanctuary with Te'Irena's curse in effect, the fire demon herself heard what the lovers had done to avoid her curse. Seeking to destroy them, but too weak to cast another incantation, Te'Irena tried to find them. However, she wandered aimlessly through the woods, in endless circles, until she stumbled upon the egg-shaped dome. She thought the edifice appalling, until she thought Te'Viro appeared and beckoned her inside. Startled and lured at the same time, she entered the C'Ovo in hopes of finding him. Tormented by her desire, her guilt, she slowly descended into madness, betrayed by her own hateful heart which could never find its place in the Infected Lovers' Paradise.

And so, Te'Kala and Letheon ruled over their secret, and forbidden sanctum until they faded into legend, burning happily with endless passion and drowning willingly deeper in love with each other.

CHAPTER 9

Swallowed by the Earth

"Ah." I set down my pen, rubbing my stiff hand to get rid of the soreness. I leaned back when the strange man popped up from underneath the large tree root I sat on, staring at me with the fascination of a curious toddler.

"I told you this place brought suffering," he whispered, eyes darting around as if he was afraid he would evoke the wrath of Te'Irena herself.

"My hand is sore because I wrote down the story you told me about this place. It's hardly suffering compared to that of the people in the tale," I said, letting the tranquility of C'Ovo interlude on our conversation.

"Why did you tell me that story? Don't misunderstand, I'm grateful you did, but why?" I sat before a beautiful clear lake, a sparkling waterfall clattering nearby. I put the notebook and pen safely away, watching the man turn over small rocks and look behind prickly bushes.

I didn't know what to expect when I was dragged into C'Ovo, but it was a truly isolated paradise within the magical forest outside. It was more humid here, like a tropical rain forest. Mist clung to the thick air, iridescent wisps floated about, changing colors when the light hit them.

"Considering that you claim to be a Collector of Stories—the good one, not the nasty one—I figured that if I helped you search for a story to collect, you might be able to help me find what I'm looking for," my strange companion said, picking up a branch from the ground, sniffing it before licking it. "Oh, tasty!" He started gnawing on it.

I blanched at that. "So, you want me to help you find someone?" I suppose I was somewhat indebted to him for the story he gave me. The least I could do was help him out with his strange quest.

"Well, I must find *something*," he said, letting out a soft shriek when a small toad with a spiky spine leapt near his feet. He stared at it a moment before waving his hand at it. "Shoo."

The toad croaked and the man jumped, letting out a feminine squeak as the amphibian hopped back into the lake.

"Can't you tell me a bit more about whatever it is you're searching for? I mean, I would like to help you, but you have to help me help you," I said. He had been clear-headed when he told me the story, so maybe he could be clear about what it was he was looking for, too.

He blinked at me, apparently dumbfounded. "But I did help you! I gave you a story to collect!" He emphasized by pointing at my backpack where my notebook was stowed. *Well, so much for clear-headed...*

"That's not what I mean. You have to tell me what you're looking for so I can help you look for it." I was only a little concerned that I was starting to get used to his manner of speech.

"Hm, perhaps we should just go looking and I'll tell you when I know you've found it?" He grinned widely.

I sighed. "I doubt that will work."

"Do you really?" He stared at me again, but I remained unfazed this time. "It's a pity," he started. "I think I would have liked it if you were the one I was supposed to find, but alas..." His voice was much lower than it had been before. His eyes darkened briefly. I leaned back from him when I felt the ground tremble beneath me.

The man pulled away as well, watching as the earth around me shook.

"What's going on?" I held onto the tree root I sat on, watching the dirt beneath me shift.

"Interesting..." He smiled when the earth stopped shaking. "It seems that Fire may have brought you here but the Earth is calling you now."

"The Earth? What are you talking about this time?" I said, quickly putting my backpack on and jumping off the root while I still could. I nearly shrieked when I felt something cold and tiny touch my ankle.

A puppet, still covered in dirt, was staring up at me. Now, I knew very well that puppets were not alive, but to see one staring at me as if it was *truly* seeing me, was beyond frightening. Though it was delicately crafted, wearing gold armor, and even bearing a golden bow on its back, I couldn't help but feel uneasy under its gaze. Its eyes were glistening black, small and narrow, peering at me. Its face was a pearly white, with a straight nose and red lips.

The puppet wore its black hair up in a bun that curved upward in a swirl. It was covered halfway by a golden headdress, etched with beautiful floral patterns. Now that I took a closer look, I noticed the quiver of arrows on its back as well. It even bore a ceremonial dagger at its waist. I recognized the puppet from ancient Asian mythology, but to find something from my world in this one was exceptionally bizarre.

"Hello," the strange man said after a long silence. "Who are you?" Curiosity laced through his voice when he cooed at the puppet.

The puppet turned its head, as if in response to the question.

I squealed. "It's alive!"

"Of course it is, why shouldn't it be?" the man asked.

"It's a puppet! Puppets shouldn't be alive!"

"All things that were created have a soul, Collector of Stories. Surely, you, who creates with words, should know this." He wiggled his eyebrows at me as if he actually knew what he was talking about for once. I, on the other hand, had nothing to say. I watched as the puppet dusted the dirt off of its clothes.

"I wonder how it got here." The man pondered, looking around.

I shuffled further away, but the puppet didn't take its eerie gaze off of me. Frowning, I noticed something laying behind it, half-covered in the dirt. Moving carefully, I grabbed the hidden object, making sure to keep an eye on the puppet. I didn't want to accidentally upset it. Ceremonial or not, that dagger looked sharp.

"E-excuse me." I cleaned the object and studied it. "Oh, pretty," I said, surprised to see how easily the dirt fell off of the white hat. It looked like something a wizard would wear. It was soft to the touch, the fabric glistening where I stroked it. However, my attention was drawn to the black star that hung at the tip of it.

I tapped the strange man on the shoulder. "Is this what you're looking for?" I asked, half in jest. But when he gazed at the white hat and the black star that dangled from the tip, he gasped, completely mesmerized.

"Hello," he said, grabbing the hat from my hands. "Who are you?"

The star chimed like a little celestial bell under his touch, softly gleaming. He grinned and set it upon his head.

"What a wonderful hat!" He stood proudly before me. "Tell me, how do I look?"

The black star bent down to dangle in front of his head instead of standing erect at the top. I took a step back to properly appraise him, and chuckled at how cheerful he looked.

"In all honesty?"

"Yes, please."

"You look like a fool, to me."

He grinned when he caught me smirking at him. He bowed gracefully before nodding at the puppet that still stood near my feet.

"Your journey is not yet finished, Collector of Stories, which is a good thing, I believe."

I looked uneasily at the puppet. "You don't mean I should follow that thing, do you?"

The puppet turned to gaze at me.

"I believe that is exactly what it wishes you would do," he answered. "However, don't despair. I feel we will meet again, one way or another. Perhaps then you will have found the person I'm looking for!"

I couldn't help but chuckle at his optimism. "Sure, I'll try my best."

"I have no doubt you will." He bowed again and I smiled at him.

The puppet had climbed onto a tree branch, from where it could tap me on the head. It pointed forward, rushing back down to lead the way.

"I suppose I have to go."

"Go, so others may come, Collector of Stories," the man said in farewell. "You'll have lots of stories to write to drive out this darkness."

My heart thumped. His voice sounded distant and deep, as if it wasn't him that said those last words. "What did you say?" I asked in a whisper.

The man was playing with the black star, a smile on his ruby lips. "Off you go, Collector! Hurry, the little puppet is leaving!"

His usual voice returned and he waved farewell. I didn't have time to mull it over, chasing after the puppet instead. I must have imagined it. It hadn't sounded like his voice and what he said didn't make sense. What darkness could he have meant?

My thoughts were interrupted when I was led out of C'Ovo, the puppet running fast for something so small.

"Wait, where are we going?" I called after the puppet as it dashed through the forest, nimble in its movements.

I ran after it as best as I could, the forest passing me in a flurry of green and brown. I noticed the slight shift in my surroundings. It was less humid here, the scent of wet earth and pines overwhelming my senses.

By the time I caught up with the puppet, my sides were burning and I pathetically panted as I watched the thing disappear into a massive cave.

"Sure, you go on ahead, I'll just take a break for a moment here."

I huffed, leaning on my knees for a bit before straightening to see where the puppet had led me to.

The cave looked to be hollowed out at the foot of a gigantic mountain, the side of it adorned by dozens of faces etched in the stone. The biggest face had sharp eyes that looked downward at its gaping mouth— the entrance to the cave. It reminded me an awful lot of the face of a carnival clown at old circuses from days gone by.

Something tugged my pants. The puppet had reappeared, pointing into the cave.

"Sorry, I'll follow you," I said, forcing my feet to move forward.

The cave was gloomy, with soft glowing moss and stalagmites and stalactites sparkling about. Small gemstones dotted the ceiling, like constellations I could put in my pocket. It was beautiful, except I couldn't help but imagine being swallowed by a gigantic mouth as I walked deeper into the mountain.

After a few minutes of walking, the puppet came to a standstill in front of a massive, black, gaping abyss. The darkness was so intense I couldn't even see the bottom. A wind howled within it and I imagined something staring back at me from the void.

The puppet tapped on a nearby stone to catch my attention before it pointed at the gorge.

"You want me to jump into that?" I asked.

The puppet nodded its head in encouragement.

"Absolutely out of the question! I am not going to jump into that thing!"

The puppet paused for a second, before drawing its golden bow and notching an arrow.

"If you want to shoot me, go right ahead. I won't feel a thing from that flimsy arrow anyway. I am *not* going to jump in there." I crossed my arms over my chest as the puppet stomped its foot, and put its weapon away. It then tugged at my pant leg, trying to drag me forward.

"I'm not jumping," I repeated, shaking the puppet away. It angrily stomped its foot again before making a dismissive gesture. Then it simply dove into the abyss.

Startled, I attempted to look down to where the puppet had fallen, hoping to catch a glimpse of its shining gold armor in the darkness. I strained to listen for the sound of a distinctive thud, but it never came.

"Are you all right in there?" I called out, though of course I shouldn't have expected an answer.

As I leaned away from the abyss, I thought I saw something stirring within the darkness. I was sure that wasn't possible—no one could see through that density.

Unable to help myself, I leaned forward again, peering into the chasm. Was I imagining things, or was something large steadily ascending from the shadows?

My gasp echoed through the cave as a gigantic, wooden hand loomed over me. Its hinges creaked as the fingers opened and moved to grasp me.

I ran the other way as fast as I could. I had nearly reached the exit of the cave when the hand closed around me and dragged me back, down into the abyss before I even had the mind to scream.

part four

Earth

CHAPTER 10
Doll House

Eyes watched me from all around the chamber. From the top to the very bottom, the shelves were filled with dolls of all shapes and sizes. I shuddered, realizing I was stuck in a catacomb of dolls. Plastic and porcelain heads in various states of decay stuck out from the dirt walls. Wooden limbs were embedded in crevices as if they tried to crawl out.

It was definitely not the kind of room I wanted to find myself in.

Served me right, I suppose, to follow a freaky puppet around. But, honestly speaking, what would you have done?

Now, I'll admit that it wasn't the best decision I made in my life, but when adventure called, I had to heed it... *Even though I might regret it just a bit right now.*

I sat on the cold floor, looking at the plethora of dolls and puppets. Some of them were eerily lit with strings of light that crossed the shelves in an attempt to brighten the room. The shadows casted on them gave off the illusion that the dolls were moving. My skin crawled.

I gazed up, my throat dry, trying to imagine how far down I was.

All I could see was massive darkness above me.

Perhaps now was a good time for a small confession, while being surrounded by inanimate objects that bore holes in my being. Their glassy, soulless eyes all seemed to stare at me, as if they knew what I was thinking, as if they could smell it.

I hate dolls.

They make me uncomfortable and anxious, and while there is some truth to all creations bearing souls, I didn't like the idea of puppets having them. There was something inherently creepy about a toy that had a human likeness, but could never truly be human.

I cried out when the puppet from earlier appeared before me, grabbing my pant leg again.

"I don't want to continue," I whispered, afraid the dolls around us would hear me.

The puppet shook its head in exasperation and tugged harder. It wasn't until I heard countless tiny whispers and giggles around me that my feet jittered and jumped into action. The puppet was disgruntled by my sudden movement but continued pulling until I moved.

"Where are we?" I asked.

The puppet answered by pointing at the hallway. Now that I looked properly around, I couldn't find the giant wooden hand that had grabbed me before. Was there something enormous waiting for me at the other end of the hall?

The string of lights sputtered above me as the scent of wood and wax prickled my senses. I finally moved, wishing for the quiet forest of floating lights, or the strange, beautiful paradise of C'Ovo. This place I roamed in now was dark and confined. I tried my best not to notice the dolls stacked against the walls, all raising their heads as I passed. An icy chill rippled through my spine, goosebumps appearing on my skin.

This was the first time during this curious, enchanting journey, that I wasn't sure whether I wanted to continue. This world was much scarier than those I had encountered before.

At the end of the hallway stood a closed door. The first thing I noticed, besides its humongous size, was the intricate detail crafted expertly into the wood. There were images of a lovely island in the middle of the ocean, followed by a large eighteenth century ship at sea. I followed the journey on the door until it ended at a room filled with more puppets and dolls. While the craftsmanship was impressive enough, the style was truly beautiful. It reminded me of artwork found uniquely in parts of South-East Asia— there was something magical, yet familiar, about this particular work of art.

"Through here?" I asked the puppet, the doubts of continuing my journey ebbing away.

The puppet nodded and I pushed against the door with my entire weight. It didn't budge. I pulled at the large, old handle. It creaked under the strain and left some rust on my hand, but the door still didn't move.

The puppet tapped impatiently against the door. I shrugged in its direction. "I can't open it."

It sighed before climbing up my leg.

"Hey! What are you doing? Get off!" I swatted at the agile puppet but it dodged my strikes, climbing up my shoulders and diving into my backpack. It rummaged through the bag before reappearing, my pen in its hands.

"What do you want me to do with that?"

The puppet pointed at the door, handing me the pen. When I grabbed it, it leapt from my shoulder to the handle of the door. The puppet hung from it for a while, swinging and kicking before jumping off.

"You want me to draw on the door? I can't do that, don't you see the craftsmanship that went into making this?" I said.

The puppet shook its head. It gestured at the handle again and pointed at the pen I was holding.

Sighing, I inspected the door a second time, finally noticing that one of the carved flowers beneath the handle looked like a keyhole.

"Oh..." I said, "You think my pen is a key? Why didn't you say so?"

The puppet clunked its hand against its head, pointing at the keyhole with some urgency.

"I don't think I can open it this way, but I'll give it a try." I pushed the pen into the keyhole, flinching at the sound of a loud clack. Having nothing else to lose, I turned the pen, stepping back as I heard gears rotating from the inside. Iron and wood screeched and the door slowly swung open.

The puppet, impatient as it was, pulled at the door as well. I was filled with trepidation, wondering what was waiting for me on the other side.

The fresh scent of pines flooded through the opening of the door. A breeze welcomed me with a gentle embrace as birds chirped in greeting. Leaves swished soothingly as I inhaled the invigorating scent of petrichor. I stepped outside into yet another forest, with soft rain falling down on me.

I was more than happy to leave the dank hallway of creepy dolls behind me, but I wasn't sure whether the lonely, colorful, caravan that stood before me would be any better. The puppet ran through the rain and the puddles toward the wooden vardo. It was mostly painted in hues of purple, blue, and gold.

The puppet climbed the steps and knocked on the door before laying down as if sleeping.

Holding my breath, I watched for the double doors to open, but when nothing happened, curiosity won me over. I approached, picking up the puppet from the floor. I knocked on the doors.

"Is someone in there?" I asked, my loud voice a stark contrast to the soothing pitter patter of the rain against the wood.

Again, there was no response. As there wasn't anyone else around, I jiggled the door handle and it opened. I knew I shouldn't have been trespassing, but considering I came this far, I thought I might as well look around.

I was not surprised to see the vardo decorated—or rather, infested—with countless dolls. They sat on the tables, hung from the ceiling, occupied most of the shelves, and some even sat on the bed.

I made a face at one particular doll that was caged in an obscure part of the room. I was struck by the bright blue eyes of despair on the puppet's face. So much so that I was already reaching out to free it.

"Ow!" I yelped, dropping the golden puppet when I felt a nasty sting. Holding out its tiny dagger, the puppet shook its head. It scaled the shelves, reached the cage, and kicked it aggressively.

"What? I just wanted to take a look," I said.

The puppet jabbed its dagger at me.

"Okay, calm down. I'm sorry. You have your reasons for keeping that doll in there, I suppose. It wasn't my place to meddle." I lifted my hands and backed away.

Satisfied by my answer, the puppet sat on a nearby shelf to keep watch of its prisoner.

"Weird block of wood," I muttered under my breath, sucking the blood clean from the tiny prick made by the dagger. Exploring further, I found a work station, peppered with remnants of wood, carving tools haplessly strewn over the desk. In a basket on the ground lay yarns of thread in different colors, pre-dominantly silver, gold, and black.

"So, someone does live here, then. A puppet maker...?" I mused, still playing with the pen in my hands as I cautiously examined the many dolls around me. I acknowledged the craftsmanship with which they were made, but due to their realism, a heavy sense of unease settled over me.

At the back wall hung masks that unnerved me even more. Hollow eyes gazed at me while I moved about the room. Some of them were crafted in the same style as the puppet in golden armor.

Despite the creepy vibes they gave off, I felt a sense of recognition when looking at them. Masks like these were typically created in the Asian archipelago known as the Emerald of the Equator. I had traveled to those islands often enough to know their culture and their land. While I didn't know how these distinctive pieces of art had gotten here, I did know that I wasn't in the tropical archipelago.

A trickle of hope rushed through me. While the locations I had traveled through so far were unfamiliar and bizarre, this place held objects that I could actually recognize. Did it mean that I was close to finding my way home?

"What is this?"

Jumping at the voice, I nearly knocked over a cabinet of puppets.

A silhouette appeared in the doorway. When the stranger stepped in, I stared at a youthful, agitated, bronzed face. Hooded eyes glared at me. His black hair was sleek, though thick, with accents of deep purple locks waving through it. He seemed to be of South-East Asian descent, and his accent was noticeable but not overpowering. He towered over me with ease, cracking his knuckles to give me a glimpse of his decorated hands, adorned with golden rings on each finger—they resembled tiny coiled ropes.

"I-I'm sorry." I was tongue-tied. "I didn't mean to intrude, but, well..."

Would he believe me if I told him a puppet had led the way to his caravan?

His deep brown eyes suddenly shifted toward me as if noticing me for the first time. "Why are you speaking? Was I talking to you?" There was a biting edge to his voice.

I was dumbfounded. "You weren't speaking to me?"

The man scoffed at me. "Why would I speak to a stranger?"

I honestly had no response to that.

The puppet got to its feet and pointed frantically at me.

"Her?" the young man said. Apparently the puppet had a way of communicating with the man that I couldn't follow. He turned and appraised me from head to toe before clacking his tongue in disapproval. "Does she look like the person I'm looking for?"

All I could do was gawk dumbly at him.

"Argh!" He squeezed the bridge of his nose, shaking his head. "She's not the one!" He made erratic gestures in my direction. "I don't care that she managed to open the door. Anyone with a stick could force the locks open!"

My eyes drifted from their bizarre one-way conversation, searching for a way out.

"A pen? What do you mean, a pen?" The man asked the puppet before facing me. I stopped shuffling to the exit.

"You have a pen?" he asked.

"Um, y-yes, I have a pen," I said, as steadily as I could.

"Why?"

"Pardon?"

"Pen! Why do you have a pen?" He gestured, his accent making each word sharper.

I shrugged awkwardly. "I like to write. I'm a writer," I explained, but the man pulled a face of disgust. He spat into a can on the floor.

Charming...

"Your stories, your writing, it's useless to me." He removed his cloak and hung it near the tiny fireplace. "Writers make more stories, they fix nothing." He spoke with a kind of cynicism beyond his age, grabbing the golden puppet from the shelf. He smacked the cage that contained the imprisoned puppet with his other hand before sitting down behind his desk to clean the remnants of dirt off the puppet.

"Well, in all fairness, writers write, we don't fix things. We're not handymen, we're creators of stories."

The young man scoffed at my words. "That's why I don't need you," he said bluntly. "I need..." He seemed to be looking for the right words to say. "I need someone who *lives* stories, not writes them." He muttered to the puppet in a language I did not understand.

"I'm sorry to disappoint then," I responded with a bite, hoping the sarcasm didn't go unnoticed. I watched him work, waiting for more.

However, he dismissed me with a wave of his hand, motioning to the door. "Go back, Writer, you're not the one I'm looking for."

"I've heard that before," I said, with a deep sigh of annoyance. "I'm starting to believe that might not be entirely true. This is *my* journey," I said, as realization slowly dawned on me.

"This is my journey, my own. If I was brought here to you, it was done so for a reason. You may not know what that reason is, and I certainly don't know what that reason is either. But if there's a story here for me to hear, then I will write it down, whether you have use for it or not."

The man clacked his tongue. "And what use will there be for you to write down these stories, hm? There's certainly no use in it for me." He crossed his arms, waiting for my response. His dark eyes shot daggers at my face.

"Your puppet seems to think differently." I nodded at the doll.

"It simply mistook you for someone else."

"It seemed very sure when it stumbled upon me."

"You are not the one I seek. I should know who I'm looking for and you, Writer, are not it." Though he snapped at me, I detected a certain air of desperation hiding behind his annoyance. "You write and tell stories, and what does that do? Nothing. Everything stands still, and I'm tired of that."

"I'm sorry to tell you this, but if there is one thing I've learned on my journey so far, it's that stories never stand still. I write stories and I hope that people read them. When they read my words they, too, can know of the worlds I've visited and learn of the stories I've collected. I was brought here seeking a story to write. Others might come here for the very same reason. Perhaps the one you're looking for is amongst them as well."

"Impossible."

The puppet then pointed at my backpack, its hand swirling in the air as though writing on invisible paper. Understanding what it meant, I grabbed my notebook and pen.

"What have you to lose?" I asked.

"A story, of course," he replied.

"But you think they have no value."

The puppet clapped its wooden hands in what I took as laughter. The young man hissed at it, before looking at me. His gaze was intense, but I remained unfazed as best as possible.

"What if I say that your journey ends here? That I have no stories for you to collect?" He slouched in his chair, a smug look on his face.

"Then I would call you a terrible liar."

"Well, I so happen to have no stories to tell." He put his hands behind his head.

"Terrible liar," I said, before pointing at the doll inside the cage. "That's a story, right there. Why don't you tell me about that?"

The young man glanced at the imprisoned puppet for a moment, a flash of anger and disgust shining in his dark eyes. "No," he answered under his breath. "That is a story for another time." He glanced back at me. His calculating stare made me uncomfortable. I jutted out my chin in response, standing my ground.

He took a deep breath as though he made up his mind. "I can tell you a different story, but you may not like it."

Masking my surprise at his sudden change of heart, I rolled my wrist in preparation. "I'd be grateful."

"Even when my story is about the death of a writer?" he said, smiling for the first time since we met. I swallowed hard and hesitated for a second, the tremble in my fingers catching his attention.

"If that is the story you have for me, then I'll take it," I answered, fighting through my hesitation.

The man watched me, his hooded eyes shone with the vaguest glint of madness before he nodded. The golden rings around his fingers started unwinding into long, shimmering rope, magically attaching them to various puppets strewn around the caravan. My eyes were wide in disbelief as he controlled the puppets' gestures and movements with delicate precision and skill, the dolls moving and speaking in his stead as they dangled in front of me.

"If it's a story you so desperately want, Writer, then let the show begin. Though do be warned, my stories are not for the fainthearted..."

CHAPTER 11
Death of a Writer

There once lived an old puppet maker, out in the middle of the forest. He spent his days chopping wood and practicing his trade. He lived in isolation, honing his skills to create beautiful, life-like puppets he would sell at the nearby town.

While he kept to himself, the villagers couldn't help but gossip about the puppet maker and his peculiar talent. His remarkable ability to carve the most realistic puppets was often the talk of the town, many claiming his skill to be inhuman, some going as far as to say that he dabbled in black magic.

These rumors ran rampant when the village suffered from a series of child abductions. Suspicions grew when the townsfolk noted each time a child went missing, the old puppet maker had produced yet another exquisite puppet. Tongues wagged viciously, claiming the old man turned children into dolls because he was unable to have children himself.

The truth, however, was far more sinister.

The puppet maker paid no mind to hearsay, though his heart ached each time there was news of another child vanishing. He knew, like no other, the pain of losing a child. No matter how many decades passed, the grief never waned, the wounds never healed. How often he wished he had paid more attention to the features of his only offspring, the details of a smiling, lively face.

His own boy had taken his pony to ride in the woods, but never came back. By the time the puppet maker found his son with a broken neck, he hardly recognized him. A passerby had covered his body with a tattered cloak, but hadn't taken the time to bury him, no one came to state they found him.

Now that he was an old widower, every day when he practiced his trade he was reminded there was no one to carry on his legacy. No matter how well he remembered the faces of the children of the village, he could hardly remember that of his own child.

"Life must go on." He woke each morning with these words on his lips and tried his best to live by them.

One day, when the news of the disappearing children had died down somewhat, the puppet maker traveled deep into the forest, searching for high quality wood for carving. He enjoyed these walks, the serenity making him feel like he owned the woods. Usually, he was the only one to pass through the quiet paths, but today the old man was taken aback to see a figure approaching him.

The old puppet maker pushed his handcrafted wheelbarrow forward, trying not to make eye contact with the drifter. However, he couldn't help but study the stranger. He had never seen the man in the village before.

The man's clothes were filthy and ragged, his hair slick with grease. A golden tooth shone prominently in the crooked grin he shot the puppet maker's way.

"Oi, old man, have you any water to spare?" the man called out, picking his teeth with a dirty knife. The man's eyes shifted to the flask that hung from the wheelbarrow.

Too nervous to deny the request, the puppet maker handed over the flask, a jitter in his fingers. As he did so, he took note of the red stains on the stranger's knife. A shiver traveled down his spine. Similar red blotches appeared on the man's clothing as well, but he seemed uninjured.

Naturally wary, the puppet maker thought about the missing children from the village. They never apprehended the person responsible for their disappearances. He swallowed.

Whose blood is he wearing?

"Much obliged, old man." The stranger grunted before dropping the flask, spilling the water over the earth near the puppet maker's feet. "Oops, sorry." The man laughed boisterously, golden tooth glinting. Then, he left.

The puppet maker felt some grim relief that all the stranger did was spill his water and not his blood.

Trying to forget the unpleasant meeting, the puppet maker quickly continued his journey, his mind spinning. Had there been talk of a drifter with a golden tooth? Travelers hardly passed by these areas, and he assumed no one from the village would harm their own children. Was the stranger simply a passerby, or did he roam these parts for more malevolent purposes?

His aged mind easily sent to a state of unrest and worry, it took the puppet maker a while to notice a red substance trailing before him. He froze in his tracks, staring at the red smudges on the wheel of his cart. He looked around and his heart raced when he saw something haplessly bundled at the side of the road.

Rushing forward, the puppet maker gasped at the murdered body of a small child.

Shaking his head, he fell to his knees, numbness enveloping him.

"No—not again!" Flashes from his past tormented his mind, his heart wrenched and a haze overcame him when he looked at the boy.

Blue, milky eyes gazed at him, ebony curls framing the child's face. When he looked long enough, the puppet maker could imagine two dimples denting the boy's chubby cheeks and the old man drew a long breath.

Was this how he looked like? My boy?

He stared at the child, images of his past still haunting his mind. How could someone not bury the body, leaving it vulnerable and disgraced for animals to gnaw on? Did anyone else know the child was here? Would his parents still be looking for him?

A sharp pain shot through his heart, the feeling of thorns coiling all around his body. He had felt the sensation before, when his hope died, his heart shattered and his mind snapped. Finding his son's dead body was the worst thing to have ever happened to him.

No parent should feel that kind of anguish.

"Yes...no...I can—" The old man ran a clammy hand through his thinning hair, finding it difficult to breathe. "My boy..." Muttering under his breath, the puppet maker gently stroked the child's face, wrapping the body properly in the cloth. "I'll fix this," he said, nodding fervently. "No pain for others, I'll carry it, yes..." He rambled, picking up the body, a twisted grimace on his face. "I'll fix this..."

Finding a secluded place, the puppet maker buried the child underneath the boughs of an old oak tree, unaware of the approaching storm. The longer he stood by the freshly dug grave, the more difficult it became for his old mind to distinguish between the memories of his past to the recent events. Had he buried another child, or another son?

The wind picked up and the rain beat down. He stood unmoving, haunted by pain. It wasn't until the lightning crackled in the air and a thunderbolt hit the oak tree, that the puppet maker woke from his reveries.

His mind cleared and he stumbled back just in time. One of the heavy branches came crashing down onto the grave of the child. He scampered to move it, grabbing a hatchet from his belt to hew into it. When he hacked into the branch for the first time, he realized what sturdy wood it was.

Gazing one more time at the grave of the little boy, his face appearing easily in his mind's eye, the puppet maker knew what to do.

Under the music of the rolling thunder, the old puppet maker wheeled a log of the broken branch back home. Once he dried the wood and prepared it, he locked himself in his house, carving it as though possessed. He labored for many a day and night, but once he was finished, he knew he had done the dead boy some justice. The life-sized puppet he had made was so beautiful and realistic, it almost felt like the child had come back to life.

"Life goes on."

The old man was so proud of his creation he started to truly adore the child-like puppet. With each passing day, he began to forget the gruesome memories from his past, more and more. He treated the object as if it were alive, and—as his old mind convinced him—why should he grieve and feel pain when he had so perfectly captured the spirit of the boy inside the puppet?

Every day, he would speak to it, clean it, take it with him on his cart when he went out into the woods to gather material for his craft. At one point, he even started feeding it, as if he was taking care of a human son.

One day, when the puppet maker was reading to the puppet, it answered him back. Stunned, the old man gazed at it, waiting to see if it would do so again. The puppet remained quiet, so he continued reading.

"Ethics are the moral principles which guide people to learn right from wrong. Now, you must always be a good boy, my son, for those who commit sins are bad and must always be punished."

"Yes...pa-pa..." Though its tongue was heavy and its speech wooden, the puppet managed to make itself heard.

Dropping the book, the old man's shock quickly turned to joy, as he deemed the sudden response a true miracle.

Day by day the puppet slowly bloomed to life, speaking broken words at first before gradually crafting whole sentences. It started moving its eyes and its head, its fingers next and then its hands. The only thing the puppet did not develop was the ability to walk, and so the puppet maker would carry the puppet on his back without complaint. He considered the puppet his son, and he would do anything to keep it pleased.

While living in blissful isolation in the forest, the puppet maker knew happiness, spending his days with his son, teaching him all he knew, as the puppet boy observed and listened.

Weeks had passed when the old man went out to collect more wood, his son sitting on the wagon.

"This won't be long, but practice your patience like a good boy," he said. "I'll be back soon."

The puppet nodded and did as it was told. Patience was a virtue, after all.

A peculiar drifter passed by in time, looking haggard and moving steadily toward the wagon.

The puppet did not move. Instead, its glassy eyes gazed soullessly at the person who stopped to admire him. The man had a shining, golden tooth in his mouth.

"What do we have here?" he slurred, inspecting the puppet with a scowl. He looked around the forest and grinned at the doll. "I reckon I can fetch a few gold coins from you. Not as good as the real thing, but it'll do." He grabbed the puppet's chin and looked closer. He pulled a face when he inspected the bright blue eyes and curly hair carved on the head. The puppet's cheeks were rosy, two dimples denting them.

"Eerie, almost like I've seen you before." He sucked at his teeth. "You're coming with me." The man lifted the puppet from the wagon.

The puppet turned its head to look at the drifter.

"Who are you?" it asked.

"What in the world?" The man dropped it to the ground and gaped at it. "A talking puppet?"

"A puppet? I'm not a puppet. Papa says I'm a boy." The puppet blinked its wooden eyelids, staring at the golden tooth in the man's mouth.

"A boy? You? You're a piece of wood, you are! Ha!" The man clasped his hands together in delight. "A moving, talking puppet! I'll make more money off of you than I would off a living child." -

"Living child?" the puppet asked. Something dark glazed in its glassy eyes.

"You don't know what that is?"

"I am alive, and I am child," the puppet said, but the man just laughed.

"Foolish piece of wood. Did the termites gnaw your brains out? Look at you!" He knocked on the puppet's head. "You're made out of wood!"

As he laughed, the puppet's demeanor changed. It looked at its own hands, wriggling the wooden fingers, comparing them to the hands of the man. The wooden boy was fascinated by the golden tooth gleaming in the stranger's mouth.

"You are not a nice man," the puppet said quietly. "There's red on your hands, and black in your heart. Your smile shines golden, but your teeth are rotten."

The thief ceased his laughter. "Say what?" He pulled a knife from his belt. "I'll saw you in half if you speak again!"

"Is your flesh soft?" The air in the woods was still and heavy. "You've asked that question to other children, haven't you?" Since the puppet could not walk, it crawled forward with its arms.

The thief stood his ground, yet his voice quivered when he spoke. "What are you, demon?"

"I am a boy. Are you a boy, or a demon?" The puppet tilted its head to appraise him, eyes gleaming a reflection of the now terrified wretch of a man. "I think I want to be like you. Soft, like you. Demonic, like you..."

Further out in the woods, the puppet maker heard the horrific screams of a horrified man crying for help. He raced back, dropping the stack of wood he had gathered, the pile clattering to the ground. What he found at the wagon shocked him to his core.

"My boy, what have you done?" he asked shakily.

The puppet sat in a pool of crimson and an icy chill traveled down the puppet maker's spine. Lumps of flesh covered parts of the puppet. He had no idea if he could clean up that much blood.

"He was mean, papa," it said without emotion, "but I fixed him now. He was bad, I saw it in his eyes. Don't worry, he won't be bad anymore." The puppet smiled for the first time, a golden tooth shining from its mouth.

The puppet maker didn't know if he was agitated because he remembered encountering this stranger before, or because he could not find any remorse for the death of the wretched man. Nevertheless, he still felt uneasy at what his son had done.

"Why did you do this, my boy?" he asked, placing the puppet back in the wagon.

"I was compelled, papa."

"By what?"

"His sins," the puppet said, its voice distorted. "Bad people must be punished, like you've taught me." The puppet tilted its head. "Did I not do it right, papa? I can do better." Its eyes glazed at him. "I can fix it."

Swallowing, the old man forced a smile. "Very well, my boy. Of course you can." It was a mistake. The puppet didn't know any better. The old man could only hope nothing so gruesome would ever happen again.

His hope was in vain.

Each time a poor, sinful soul stumbled upon the puppet, it never let them leave. Each time it claimed a life, it stated it was doing something good, ridding the world of bad people.

Somewhere, the puppet maker knew he should burn the puppet, his son, but his delusional love prevented him from doing so. He told himself repeatedly the puppet did no harm to good folk. It only harmed those with black hearts and evil souls. There was some good in that, wasn't there?

The old woman that crossed their path was a terrible witch that loved to torment animals. The young man was an adulterer and had abandoned his children. The woman that roamed the woods was one that roamed the streets, selling herself to the highest bidder. These were cads and villains and bad people, but the line between good and bad blurred further with each passing day.

The puppet maker came to this chilling realization whilst crying over the lifeless body of a beautiful young maiden, whose only sin was to have been born with angelic looks.

"Papa, it is bad to be that vain, isn't it? She looked only at herself in the river and would not even acknowledge me. What if I needed help? So selfish... She twirled her hair and played with it all the time, though I agree her hair is quite soft."

To his horror, the old man saw how strands of hair and chunks of flesh had begun to sprout from the puppet's head. Its appearance had grown more grotesque— human characteristics mixing with the wood. With each life it took, the puppet seemed to appear more human. But in the eyes of its maker, it only looked more like a monster, mirroring the wretchedness of its victims.

Plagued by guilt and numb helplessness, the puppet maker did the only thing he could to cope: he carved. He recreated all the people his puppet had slaughtered, in perfect detail, and left them at the edge of the village. He hoped it would bring some comfort to those who saw them. For, try as he might, he had no courage, nor strength, to destroy his puppet.

Time passed without bloodshed and the puppet maker grew hopeful the puppet had sated its bloodlust. However, as he was still reluctant to leave the puppet home alone, he took it with him to the forest when he needed to gather more wood.

"Stay here, I'll be back swiftly." He left after ensuring the puppet couldn't leave.

An hour passed when a wandering boy happened to stumble upon the cart, running toward it.

"Hello? Is someone there?" the boy asked. He curiously looked into the cart and climbed in, too late to see he wasn't alone.

The puppet turned its head, noticing how perfectly human the boy was. It studied its own appearance, the wooden fingers with bits of flesh, touched one eye made of glass and one that wasn't. The puppet had first looked at the boy to uncover his sin, but now it compared itself to the child.

A new desire overwhelmed the creature.

"Oh, what are you?" The boy picked up a stick, gazing at the puppet, unaware the puppet maker had returned.

The old man blanched at the movements he saw in his cart. He watched, in horror, as the small, curious boy poked the monstrous puppet with a branch.

He saw the puppet drawing the child closer, its eyes gleaming in a way they never had before. Its hands reached for the boy and with all the strength he possessed, the old puppet maker ran toward the cart, scooping up the unsuspecting boy before the puppet could touch him.

"Enough!" he exclaimed, setting the startled boy down. "You go back to the village and do not dare to ever return! Say it to all those who will hear it: If you value your life, do not enter these woods!"

Scared out of his mind, the boy fled for his life.

"Why did you do that, papa? I only wanted to play with him. I wanted to ask what it was like to be so soft...and human." The puppet garbled in an unfamiliar voice. It broke the old man's heart in two.

"I know, son, I know all too well..."

"You wouldn't do something bad to me, would you, papa?" the puppet then asked, as though it could sense the decision the old man had made for himself.

"Of course not." The puppet maker spoke flatly. He grabbed the puppet and walked deeper into the forest.

"You know that bad people need to be punished. A man should be good and just, like you. You take care of me, you love me like your own son. Wouldn't it be nice if I was soft like one, papa?"

"Sometimes, bad children need to be punished, too." It was the only thing he could say.

They entered a dark part of the forest, where the leaves grew so thick the sun could not pierce through. There were ancient caverns here, known only in the village folktales and said to be cursed, which only burdened the puppet maker more when he placed his son in one of the caves.

"I'm sorry." The old puppet maker looked at his once beautiful creation. He couldn't help but shudder at his own reflection shining in the puppet's eyes. "No one will find you here. I-I have to fix this. It's better this way."

Straining himself, he pushed a boulder in front of the entrance of the cave and abandoned his creation. He hoped that no one would fall prey to it again. He left with a heavy heart, his adage weakly leaving his lips.

"Life goes on."

Weeks later, while the puppet maker was working on another doll, a storm rushed over the lands. He had grown accustomed to the silence, and greeted loneliness like a prodigal son. He stretched his sore, creaking body, cursing his old bones.

A knock on his door surprised him, given the late hour and the fact that had he never received visitors before. Curious, he went to open it.

"Hello, papa." The grotesque monstrosity of wood and rotting flesh stood framed against the dark, brooding skies. "Look! I'm real now, so I've learned to walk!" The creature dragged itself inside, heavily shuffling one foot after the other. "Oh, papa, you've done a bad thing. How could you abandon your only son?"

"No..." The puppet maker shook his head, numb with fright. "No," he whispered, sinking down to his knees.

"It's not the first time you were bad. I saw your sins. How selfish of you to bury the body of that boy that looks like me and how you kept it a secret all this time. How arrogant of you to presume you knew better." The puppet smiled, the golden tooth gleaming. "And what did you do when you crossed paths with a child murderer? Nothing."

It moved closer. "But it's all right, papa. I learned my sense of justice from you. I know the right from wrong even if you don't anymore." The puppet approached his father, moving closer and closer. "Shall I teach you instead?"

There was once a puppet maker that lived in an old, decrepit shed in the middle of the forest. He made a puppet that came to life and found a way to be real. Now his hollowed body hangs under thrall, with the puppet forever pulling on his strings...

It is said that those with wretched souls may meet a similar fate. The puppet may see what's in your blackened heart, and has grown an appetite for the taste of bad blood. So you'd best beware and be warned: Live your life well, honestly, and selflessly, or the hungry puppet might take your soul.

Taking a deep, much needed breath, Raku set his pen down and stretched his hand and fingers. The writer reread the last paragraphs he had written and nodded, satisfied. The story of the puppet maker and his monstrous puppet had been nagging at his brain for days now. He was relieved he could finally finish it.

As the writer stretched himself, he noticed a figure sitting in the distance, clad entirely in black—staring at him.

Raku couldn't see the figure's face, concealed as it was by a hood, but he knew he was being watched. Undisturbed by the mysterious figure's presence, Raku went about his own business.

He took a deep breath of fresh forest air, taking a moment to enjoy the sound of leaves dancing in the wind. The sun was setting, pastel colors streaked across the sky. The mountain top peeked through the green horizon of trees like a silent guardian.

It was serenely quiet in the woods and Raku preferred it that way. He was in no mood to strike up a conversation with the stranger, and instead started to collect his belongings. The writer was quite content to be able to write the stories that had been spinning in his head in the silence of these woods.

Not many people visited the forest. It was believed to be haunted, its soil drenched with too much blood to be deemed a place of safety and good fortune. To Raku, however, it felt like home. Perhaps the forest *was* haunted, the figure in black an example of its terror. Raku did not acknowledge the figure, but he did notice a searing pain in his chest, which seemed to grow more intense when the stranger was near. Coughs racked his body.

The next day, Raku would write his gruesome fairytales which he held dear to his heart, ignore the stranger, and leave again. In the following week, Raku would repeat the same pattern, with the stranger sitting closer and closer with each passing day.

It wasn't until Raku suffered another coughing fit, covering his mouth with a bloodstained cloth, that the stranger moved right in front of him, staring. In spite of this, Raku grabbed his notebook and started writing, ignoring his odd companion, like he did all those days before. Without glancing at the stranger, he took deep, heavy breaths that pressed against his chest while he created his stories.

His time was nearly up, but there were still so many stories that he wanted to write. He needed to bring them into the world, even if it meant he risked leaving the world himself.

The silent figure sat right in front of him and as the day passed, Raku worked patiently on another story, until finally, the stranger in black finally reached their limit.

"How long do you plan to avoid me?" the stranger asked with an icy, feminine voice, the robes of her cloak waving as if they were woven by delicate mist.

Raku said nothing, not even bothering to glance up at her as he continued writing the final paragraphs.

"You write of me so often, but when I appear before you, you give me no quarter! Am I not even worth a glance?!" The stranger was used to having people respond with fear and respect, not this silent impertinence.

The writer still did not respond, though another coughing fit overwhelmed him, his breathing becoming ragged as he continued scribbling.

"You realize, even if I have to reap your soul, your presence on this earth will still have meaning in the future, long after you've perished?" The stranger had often found that mortals thought the idea of metaphoric immortality quite appealing. Perhaps she could get a rise out of him.

When the writer suddenly stopped writing, her black lips broke into a smirk. "These lands you so loyally visit have absorbed part of your essence. I am gracefully giving you the knowledge that even after death, you will leave part of your spirit behind. Are you not grateful?" she asked, growing more frustrated as the writer continued working.

"The audacity! You would even ignore Death when she stands

before you?" Black, misty wings appeared from her back, a silver scythe with an amethyst blade materializing in her bony hand. Her skin was pale, a nearly translucent contrast against the shroud of black she wore.

While others would have found the reveal shocking and impressive at the very least, Raku still did not look up from his work, leaving Death staring blankly at the mortal.

Raku finished his writing, humming to himself, satisfied. He took another deep breath, savoring the scent of his beloved forest and closed his notebook. At long last, he looked at Death, who seemed startled that he did so. She quickly recovered, attempting to impress him with her black, wide wings and gleaming scythe.

There were no emotions in the writer's face. His dark, narrow eyes betrayed nothing, though there was a sheen of sweat on his forehead. Instead, he stroked the cover of his beloved notebook, before handing it to Death.

Surprised at the mortal's odd behavior, Death tentatively took the writer's book. The moment she did so, the writer closed his eyes as though he went to sleep.

Certain that she hadn't reaped his soul, Death scoffed, dismissing her scythe. She stroked the front of the book as he had, sensing vague impressions of memories and emotions of an extraordinary life lived without excitement.

"I cannot be bought, nor persuaded, Mortal. When your time is up, there is no fighting fate."

Death inspected the book and smelled it, cringing as the scent of blood, sweat, and tears filled her nostrils. She sighed deeply, looking at the book.

She opened it.

Barely had she flipped a page when the ground shook with such a deep, angry rumble that Death rose, her wings flaring open once more. Around her, peculiar contraptions rose from the deep earth. She realized she floated in the center of a small fairground. In all her centuries of collecting souls, she had never seen something like this before.

Four attractions had risen from the earth, and while they appeared dirty and a little worn, they seemed to be fully functioning.

Death glanced at the rides in fascination and confusion. A merry-go-round rotated as organ music whined out of a scratchy speaker. The Ferris wheel stood out like a sore thumb amongst the tall, green trees, the light bulbs of the ride dull and fluttering.

There was a strange sense of irony when Death gazed upon the Haunted House attraction, a sardonic smile playing on her black lips as a fake, skeletal version of herself graced the front of the house.

Her deep purple eyes glanced at the last attraction which appeared to be a boat ride, that led into a dark cave.

In the middle of all of these peculiar happenings, Raku still sat motionless, eyes closed peacefully.

"What have you planned, Mortal? Did you sell your soul to conjure this magic?" Death asked mockingly before she fell silent as the grave, another thought entering her mind. *Or did you break your soul apart?* She flipped through the pages of the book to find it practically empty, save for the very first page.

You cannot start a story at the end.

To begin, you must start where you found me, and what you assume you know about me; a writer, who writes, every single day, like clockwork.

Death frowned at the still form of the writer, cursing him for making her job so much more complicated than was necessary.

Clockwork?

Death listened to the merry-go-round music. "If you wished me to start at the carousel, you could have said so," she said, as the ride slowed down to a halt.

"What? You wish me to ride each of these attractions? What an utter waste of time," she began, before the book opened of its own accord.

If you wish to collect my soul, you must find every part of me within these rides.

Death groaned, and found a black carousel horse to sit on. While she saw no use in this, fascination sparked her senses when the carousel started to move. The paintings of fairytales on the roof and pillars slowly came to life. The lights blinked and intensified, the colors of the ride expanding, as if the carousel was covered by a magical dome. It gave the illusion that she had been transported to another world. Death found herself sitting on a mechanical horse, moving through a disenchanted forest.

A little girl, wearing a crimson hood skipped through a dark and foreboding grove. A hungry wolf peeked at her from behind the barren trees, eyes glowing. The wolf followed the girl, but as the carousel continued moving, it became clear it was not the wolf that did the hunting.

She watched a monstrous mermaid seduce an unsuspecting prince before dragging him down into the treacherous sea. Death also saw seven, misshapen men preying on a maiden with hell red lips and skin as white as snow. Death even gasped when that same maiden turned into a ghost, dragging the seven men with her into her grave in the apple orchard.

These must be the dark and morbid fairytale stories Raku created...

Death was familiar with the sight of someone's impending demise, but this was different. At one point, the music and moving images around her seemed so real it felt like she had ended up within the pages of a book, watching each story unfold. Death was impressed by the creativity of the stories. She noticed that most of them were driven by intense pain, fear, suffering and solitude. This was not uncommon for her to see. There was no mortal on earth without those emotions. Why the writer would choose to show her this was a mystery.

Nevertheless, she found a piece of his soul pouring out of a fountain pen amidst the moving images. The merry-go-round started to slow down.

"Why are you postponing the inevitable?" Death asked, as the ride ground to a halt. "No matter what you show me, I will still collect the pieces of your soul. There is no escape."

The writer's book opened again.

I cannot cheat Death, but I'll not have Death cheat me, either.

I expect you to catch me when I fall...

The sound of the rickety Ferris wheel creaking caught Death's attention. She gazed up the towering contraption, when the ghostly apparition of a young boy dashed past her. He climbed into one of the carts and the Ferris wheel moved him up with a groan. Something stirred within her when she saw the little boy, though she couldn't explain the sensation.

It seemed like the boy beckoned her, and Death stepped into the next cart that halted before her with a creak. The cart swung gently, red paint flaking, revealing rust and corrosion of the metal. The safety bar was in an equal state of disrepair. Colored in gold and black they looked like candy stripes, but the metal was dented and brittle to the touch.

Death wasn't sure whether the contraption would be able to move without toppling over, but it took her into the sky. The wind brought a chill to her bones that she allowed to affect her for once, and the forest lay bare before her. She gazed at a sea of endless trees, dense and thick, their leaves bending and rustling, moving like the waves of a green ocean.

She kept an oblique eye on the boy who sat a few carts above her. When she leaned forward and looked up, she could see him, watching the forest.

"Why would you show me this? You're naught but a child now," she whispered at the soul. As if he heard her, the child leaned over the safety bar of the cart to look dismally at her. The cart rocked back and forth dangerously as he stood.

Even though he was small and young, Death easily recognized the dark, hooded eyes that angled upward like a teardrop curve, the mess of wavy brown hair. The child version of the writer spread his arms, closed his eyes, and teetered on the edge of the cart. Then, without a word, he jumped, plummeting to the ground.

The odd sensation Death had felt earlier returned in full force when the boy's form flashed past her. Time slowed and she caught a glimpse of his deep brown eyes before he continued falling. Startled at the agony a child could feel at such a delicate age, Death spread her wings and dived, only pulling up once little Raku was safely in her arms.

She hugged him to her chest, knowing she had collected another piece of Raku's soul. While the boy disappeared, the Ferris wheel started to turn faster. The light bulbs flickered, and she saw the ghostly apparition of the boy again, showing her how he wished he could fly away, to soar toward a better place.

But, he ended up falling further instead.

Death watched as more apparitions appeared within the carts of the Ferris wheel. Each of them jumped down when they arrived at the very top.

"We cannot all fly through life, Mortal," Death said, as the attraction filled itself with the haunting images of the fairytales Raku wrote, the characters he portrayed as his inner child. She saw the old puppet maker, a lifeless puppet—perfectly carved—sitting on his lap. A bruised, young woman sat in the cart above, holding a broken glass slipper. In another cart sat a young maiden, reading a book, her beautiful face hidden behind a horrid beastly mask.

The book opened once more, and Death read the next instruction. A strange feeling of attachment to the writer's stories crept up inside of her, or was it a growing attachment toward Raku himself? Death shook her head. She had no possible reason to feel so much trepidation for a mere mortal.

And yet...

She gazed at the book.

All my life I have been haunted, by living ghosts...

Death looked up at the facade of the Haunted House. Despite the insult of having her comical image dangling at the front of the decrepit ride, she still made for the coffin-shaped cart.

The ride screeched and rattled as the door of the dilapidated house creaked open. The house was drearily lit, doors breathing dead life. Walls with eyes followed her slow start. A loud waltz played—a haunting tune—as the cart traveled further through the dark and dirty house.

She moved past the writer's childhood room where he spent his early days writing stories, pen glued to his hand. His mechanical head turned towards a terrifying black door, as loud, thunderous sounds drowned out the eerie waltz.

Death was swallowed by darkness, though Raku's beating heart glowed erratically like a firefly in the night, guiding the way to the next scene. Having recognized part of the writer's soul within the beating heart, Death gathered it, suddenly overwhelmed by feelings of pure fear and desperation which the soul poured into her. Worry for what she would see in the next scene stole over her. She heard loud shouting and glass smashing before the door even opened.

A man and a woman were arguing with each other, the quarrel so heated that, in the subsequent scene, the man turned into a horrid monster. The mechanical behemoth slammed the crying woman down a flight of stairs, Death's cart following her descent with blinding speed. At the bottom of the stairs the woman's body lay like a rag doll, limbs bent in crooked, unnatural angles.

Little Raku cowered in a corner, unable to look away from his broken mother. Death remembered all the souls she reaped, and this woman was no exception. The memory was still vivid in her mind as she looked upon the scene now. A depiction of her fake, skeletal-self pulled the woman's soul out of her broken body, exactly as she remembered doing. What she did not recall was Raku tugging at her robe, his face beaten and bloodied, the male monster still clawing at him.

The ride ended with the boy running off into the haunted woods, where he hid from his monster father. Death bent her head when the cart approached the exit. The monster dangled there from a thick rope, tied around the scythe of yet another mechanical version of Death. The monster slowly reverted back to his human form.

Unsure why she felt shaken, Death climbed out of the car, glancing at the motionless form of the now grown writer at the center of the attractions. She still sensed the helplessness from the part of the soul she had collected, and was surprised to feel herself trembling. Perhaps ferrying the souls of mortals for all these centuries was starting to take a toll on her. She never usually felt this emotional—

unless something else was at play here...

"Not all people have a happy home," she said softly, before forcing herself to remember that Raku's tragic life was no different to that of others. "But if it is any consolation to you, I do remember reaping your mother's soul. Hers was tortured, but gentle. Your father I did not take, though I remember being present when he ended his miserable life. A colleague took him, for his sins in life were too great, and he needed to repent." Souls that were headed to the flames were not hers to collect. She would never want to ferry one of them to that dismal place, either.

Death's gaze turned to the last attraction. She was already holding out the book in her pale hands, her fingernails glittering like black diamonds. When it opened, she read the words on the page once more.

While others had the safety of boats in life's river, I did not even have the satisfaction of drowning. But I soon realized I did not need a boat to prevent me from drowning. It was a pen that saved me from the water...

"I see. I know what you mean, Writer, but I cannot extend your life, as I have said. No matter how painful, no matter how tragic it has been, I cannot grant you more life. Your life is done, there is no more left."

The book shook in her hands, the pages flipping again.

One more story.

Death took a deep breath and nodded at the still figure of the writer. "Very well. Who am I to deny the wishes of the dying?" She resisted the urge to roll her eyes and walked to the last attraction.

Unlike the other attractions, the boat ride seemed pleasant, relaxing, even. Though the water was filled with algae and the facade of the attraction was less than impressive, the boat itself looked like an elegant gondola. A lonely, candlelit lantern dangled at the front.

The vessel docked near the entrance of a purple cave. Damages on the cave revealed it to be artificial, but the darkness within the tunnel didn't give anything away.

The wind blew again, ripples forming in the midnight blue water. Death stepped onto the gondola and it moved forward, entering the dark cave. The tunnel was bare, nothing but gloomy light illuminating the blank rock walls. A soft piano started playing out of nowhere. A voice scratched around Death as shadow puppetry appeared on the cave walls.

"Once upon a time, there was a young boy that lived a life of misery," a disembodied voice narrated. "Though he never understood why life hated him so, he was at least thankful for the brief moments where he experienced being loved." Two shadow figures, little Raku and his mother, embraced one another.

"When love was taken away from him, there was little else for the writer to live for."

The puppets showed Raku in his teenage years, ostracized by classmates, and always on the run. A grownup version of the writer drifted around, no place to call home, no one to accompany him, save for the procession of his personal demons behind him.

Death felt an odd shiver roll down her spine. She had expected this collection not to be as simple as others, but there was a strange force at play now. She thought she had sensed it earlier on, but dismissed it for sentiment. Now, she couldn't rightly tell whether it was the magic spell of the writer's storytelling, or something... else.

"One day, while strolling through a sea of trees, notorious for their hauntings and cursed lands, the writer met an unusual, exceptional, man."

Death narrowed her eyes at the shadowy depiction of a creature in a top hat, with hollowed eyes and a large grin, a star shining in one cheek.

"He handed the writer a pen, of all things, a pen he claimed possessed the powerful magic to write a thousand stories. And if by chance the pen was used by an innocent, yet tortured soul, it had the ability to bring life..."

Death dropped Raku's book. Fear was such a peculiar feeling to her. She was not at all used to the emotion, but the story of the stranger and the pen... She knew that story, that ancient, long forgotten lore.

"Impossible," she whispered, looking to the next wall. The shadows showed the silhouettes of various fairground attractions.

"For the first time in his life, the writer had meaning," the disembodied voice continued. "Each story he created came to life. He scribbled the days away in his forest, feeling fulfilled now that he had a task and could leave his mark on this world."

The boat stopped in front of an extraordinary gate. It looked ancient, with odd symbols, objects, and fables etched into the metal and stone.

How, she wondered, could a mortal know of this wretched gate?

Death was so vexed by what the ride revealed to her, she almost forgot to collect the last part of the writer's soul, revealing itself in the lantern of the boat when the gate opened to continue the ride.

A shadow of herself floated by over the cavern walls, before the shadow puppet of Raku was shown again, scribbling furiously in the forest. The woods around him appeared to grow, and more attractions sprouted from the ground as he wrote in his notebook.

"The mysterious man appeared to the writer a second time." The figure with the top hat popped into being once more. "This time, it was to warn him that Death would soon claim him, but he should not worry. The pen he had been given would grant life everlasting.

He told the writer to continue his craft and to follow his instructions when Death appeared."

As it dawned on Death what Raku had done and how he was able to conjure up such ancient magic, she shook her head. "How could this man warn you of my coming? No one knows when I arrive!" She apprehensively watched the last projection of shadow puppetry.

"To do as the mysterious Samaritan told him, the writer used his pen to write down his own story. By doing so, he literally poured his soul into his work, becoming one with his scribbles. For those who are written into books, receive eternity. Immortality. This enchantment allowed the writer to split his soul in four, and the lands were spellbound with the magic created by the pen and the writer's sacrifice. It was a great price to pay, binding himself to his stories, but he could continue doing the one thing he loved doing in this world. Even in death, he could not bear the thought of never being able to write again."

The ride started to tremble, the light of the lantern turning a horrid purple and green. The shadow of the man in the top hat gleamed within and the voice of the narrator changed.

There was another scratch in the air, followed by a distorted garble. The pleasant voice suddenly sounded more chilling, more sinister. It spoke its words slowly, with a sultry lilt that carried the words like a song.

Death summoned her scythe to her hand, that velvet voice triggering a deep sense of fear within her. She was Death herself! Little could rattle her. But that terrible voice, that horrid gate... She had merely assumed they were ghosts of a past, lost in oblivion. Evidently, she was wrong.

The voice chuckled as it continued the story.

"Thus, the dear, desperate writer danced to my tune. For if he would continue to write his delicious stories, new energy and life would be in my grasp forever." The voice cackled as shadows danced erratically on the stone walls, snuffing out lights, a rumble quaking through the cave.

Death gasped as the shadows shaped and formed before her, revealing a silhouetted face on the wall. The eyes were outlined, glowing red, the grin stretching wide. His next words caused Death to flare her wings out.

"The opening of the gate is imminent..."

The boat ride ended as it steered into the light of the exit, where Death heard carnival music playing from all corners of the woods. The sun was setting and the lights of the attractions fluttered. The ground seemed to move in gentle, subtle waves beneath Death's feet, the air trembling around her.

Could Raku truly not have known that he cursed this wretched land?

Death looked at the separate pieces of the writer's soul, floating like wisps of light over the palm of her pallid hand. It explained why she couldn't feel warmth emanating from it. She released the soul.

The essence returned to its body, and Raku took a deep breath. He blinked in confusion, before steadily meeting Death's gaze. The fairground around them, however, remained.

"It worked," he muttered. "How did it feel when I ignored you?" he suddenly asked, before Death could explain what he had really done.

"What?"

"You asked me how long I was going to ignore you, you seemed agitated when I did so, but you still don't see?"

"I see a young, talented man, who squandered not only his life, but his death as well."

The writer shook his head, disgruntled. "I asked for you to get me, multiple times throughout my life," he said in accusation. "But you never came."

"It was not your time," Death answered.

The cackle of the sultry voice within the cave echoed around them like ghostly whispers. She knew Raku's fate was sealed. She was unable to do anything.

"You ignored me, all those times! You saw what kind of life I lived. Now that I found my purpose, now that I found happiness in my stories, you decide to come for me? I couldn't let that happen." Raku spoke heatedly, pulling out a pen cut from various gemstones from his coat.

"He was right. This pen can bring life to anything and anyone. You couldn't reap me, because you can't touch me unless I want you to." He grinned triumphantly, but Death only sighed.

"I cannot reap you because you were misled by a man whom is neither dead nor alive. You are not alive, Writer, and therefore you cannot die. You are not dead, because I can never claim your soul again, not even if you beg me to come get you to bring peace and relief from this world." Death spoke with pity, handing him his notebook again.

"What do you mean?" Raku asked, stroking the cover of his precious book, the pen already itching in his hand.

"He tricked you, your so-called Samaritan. Your spirit, your endless stories, are seeped within these grounds like blood watering the earth. I can never collect your soul because he is the one who will collect it instead. And once he does, you'll wish for death." She spread her magnificent black wings.

The writer wriggled his fingers and touched his face. He felt no different, but Death did not appear to be interested in collecting his soul anymore, which awakened a sense of dread.

"You won't collect my soul?"

"I *cannot* collect your soul."

"But, I can still write?"

Death shook her head, unable to fully tell him the consequences of his foolish actions.

"Even if I did attempt to stop you, you'll still be able to write," she said. Her heart nearly bled at seeing how much joy that brought the writer. If that was the only relief she was ever able to give him, then that would have to do.

"Do not let your stories consume you, Writer. It is easy to let them swallow you up, but do not let them take someone else, too. You'll bear that cross forever."

The circus music grew louder, thickening the air with the haunting melody.

"Goodbye, I fear we'll never see each other again, Raku." Death spoke solemnly, with a finality that expected no answer.

The writer's mind was already wandering to the next story he would be writing. The organ music swelled, the fairground attractions moved and whirred around him. For a moment, Raku savored the sights, happy to live.

"And thus, the writer's curse was completed, the bargain sealed."

Startled, Raku looked around for the voice that had bellowed over the circus music.

"The writer would be bound to me, now both life and Death touched his soul. Death has seen and followed my dear *Rakugo's* journey, and that was all that was needed to keep his soul tethered in between earth and the world of spirits."

The smile on the young writer's face faded, the once friendly voice sounding so menacing now.

"He would write me stories to collect, for all eternity, sending out more darkness into worlds for me to possess, until I find freedom from my bonds."

Raku turned around, but saw no one. His eyes followed a shining black feather that fell from the sky and landed on the ground. He bent to pick it up, and the silhouette of a man in a top hat loomed over him.

Raku was never seen again.

It is said that though the writer was nowhere to be found, odd and old attractions would sprout in the woods where he loved to write. If you wander in the sea of trees one day and hear the sound of circus music, you would be wise not to follow its beautiful and alluring

melody. You might end up in a story without an ending...

CHAPTER 12
Darkness Comes

The Raku puppet held up his wooden hand to his face, trying to shield himself from the shadow looming over him, growing bigger and darker, until it swallowed him whole.

The young puppeteer ended his story there, leaving me with an uneasy feeling in my stomach as I looked at my writing in the notebook.

"Wait. That's it? That's the end?" I asked in disbelief. "There has to be more!"

The puppeteer shrugged. "Like what?" He leaned back in his chair, the make-shift puppet theater having vanished.

"Like, who the top hat freak is? Or, maybe, I don't know, telling people what happened to Raku?"

"Freak, huh?" The young man raised his eyebrow. "You're a writer. You never heard of open endings?"

I scoffed at this before gently rotating my wrist. My hand was shaking, my fingers so stiff I had to let go of my pen. It rolled off my lap, but before I could grab it, the puppeteer's nimble hand had already snatched it up, the golden ropes coiled like rings around his fingers again.

"It's interesting how a small tool like this can create immortality, isn't it?" he mused more to himself, before handing the pen back to me.

The puppeteer bore an unnervingly relaxed smile on his face. "You look a little rattled, Writer. Did my story scare you?" He tipped his chair backwards so he could lean and place his feet up on his work desk. The dolls around us shook as if they were giggling.

"No," I started, rereading a few sentences on the page. "It's curious, though. This man in your story, the one in the top hat, he collects writers?" I closed the book and placed it in my backpack.

"Stories," he corrected, before shrugging again. "Same difference." He reached for something on a shelf, revealing a set of shadow puppets, from the likes of the islands in the Pacific Ocean I had traveled to. What was the term for those puppets again?

"*Wayang*," I muttered and caught his eyes gleaming at me. He stopped playing with the puppets. Was there a glint of recognition shining in his eyes?

Exactly how far away from home am I? I wondered. This world I was in now didn't seem to differ all that much from mine. Things seemed less foreign here, and looking around the vardo, I recognized some of the puppets. Ballerinas and harlequins, pirates and sailors, even kings and queens, with their jesters. Traveling through the other worlds had been so much more bizarre and unfamiliar.

"Where are you from?" I asked him.

He was muttering in his own tongue at the shadow puppets, but at my words he stopped his movements altogether, a distant look appearing in his dark eyes. He set the leather shadow puppets down with a quiver in his fingers, glaring at the puppet inside the cage. I knew there was another story there, but something told me I could ask him about it until I had no voice left to speak, and he still wouldn't tell me.

"I am lost, like you," he said, "though, you wander and are closer to your home than I am." He turned back to the golden puppet. He nodded to it, listening to words I couldn't hear.

"You must go," he suddenly said, getting to his feet, peeking outside. "There's a storm coming, and if he knows you were here, you might be collected too, Writer." The warning lingered when thunder rolled in the darkened sky.

"You're talking about that man? Who is he?" I asked. "Before, I was somewhere with a very peculiar fellow and he spoke of another Collector of Stories. Is he one and the same?"

"You really are a wanderer," he said, before chuckling. "You have no idea what awaits, do you?"

The thunder crashed, a bolt of lightning flashing through the gray clouds. Rain started to hammer on the wooden roof of the caravan.

"What awaits?" I looked out the window a moment, the rain hosing down like a waterfall. The lightning flashed, but I startled from the look on the puppeteer's face. The dim glow of oil lamps, which I hadn't noticed before, cast strange shadows on his face, as if puppets had started dancing over it.

"Darkness comes," he whispered.

The dolls began to tremble. I heard their tiny voices squeaking, wood and porcelain clattering against each other. What unnerved me further was the sound of an accordion playing through the storm.

"Why do you think you were brought here?" The puppeteer approached me, but I had no immediate answer. I walked backwards until I hit the door, but it flung open, and I stumbled out into the middle of the pouring rain, the wind of the storm picking up. The rain soaked my clothes in a matter of seconds, the wind whipping my hair, sticking to the side of my face.

The accordion music grew louder.

"I like to think I had a purpose coming here, collecting stories and going on an adventure I can call my own!" I had to yell through the storm.

The puppeteer laughed at my answer. He followed me out into the rain, and only now did I realize the storm didn't seem to affect him. The rain fell on him, but slid off, keeping him dry, almost as if he, himself, was a puppet covered in wax.

"The worlds you visited are dying," he said. "They thought your light could help fend off the darkness of oblivion that descends on these lands, but I see no greatness in you."

My chest tightened. *Dying?*

The earth trembled, the sky cracking open with a flash of purple lightning. The rain beat down on me, my feet sinking in the muddy forest floor. The circus music played through the orchestra of the storm, as a large, worn out fairground attraction emerged from the dirt.

My heart thundered in my chest as a pair of large, glowing eyes rose from the mud. Metal wings creaked under strain as the contraption continued rising, looming over me. I scrambled away. The animatronic dragon looked fierce, but ragged and rusty, dragging a train of other dragons around on a circling track.

I fell when another attraction emerged, the mud and the rainwater pooling around me.

A black fire stood in the center of a brightly colored carousel. Water could not douse it. I watched breathlessly as thirteen masked figures danced to the accordion's music, which had turned into a dark waltz. Panic raced through me, and I tried hard to break free, but the mud sucked at my body and the water level rose. The relentless stream of rain washed over me.

Was the puppeteer the one that summoned these attractions? He didn't seem like he was responsible for them. But the alternative option was even more ludicrous!

Am I doing this?

"I told you to leave when you had the chance, Writer," said the puppeteer over the storm. "I told you that you could not help me."

A large, decrepit gate made its ascension from the mud unto the surface of the earth. Gears whirred and clanked. Symbols and intricate etchings, decorating the stone and metal, lit up when the rain washed the dirt away. My gaze turned to the puppeteer, his story still fresh in my mind.

Was he the man in the top hat? He couldn't be...

"Your stories will end here, Writer. How can you create light in worlds that are already dying?" he asked, and I was surprised to hear the fragile tone in his voice, to see the look of helplessness on his face. He wasn't lying to me. How could he? Why would he?

"Are you the other collector? Are you the man in the top hat?" I shouted, trying to keep my head above the rising water.

"No," he answered solemnly, looking behind him toward a black shadow moving through the trees. A whimsical circus tune mixed with the dark waltz played louder, and louder, the music turning more sinister and out of tune.

"He is approaching. You can't help me, Writer, but, perhaps..."

The puppeteer looked frightened. Genuine fear slid over his face like a mask, as the golden puppet appeared by his side, tugging frantically at his clothes. He listened to the silent words of his golden companion.

"You better be right about this, Arjuna," he told the puppet, before approaching me. He grabbed my hand and pulled me up until our faces were inches away from each other. I gazed into his deep brown eyes that looked so...old, all of a sudden.

"I still believe you can't help me, but Arjuna seems to think otherwise. That's why I'll help you this once. I can only hope you'll repay the favor one day, Writer."

The shadow loomed ever closer.

"Write," the puppeteer urged. "We'll be waiting."

Before I could even make the promise, he dunked me back into the mud and water, further and deeper than before. My outcry was lost in the storm as my head went under. The only thing I could see through the murky water was the vague outline of the puppeteer, a shadow slowly shrouding him.

I sank deeper into a watery void. I felt the heavy substance of mud slipping away from me, swallowed whole by the water.

I floated in the abyss, unable to breathe, unable to find a way to break to the surface. Everywhere I looked I saw darkness, the cold grip of fright creeping up on me, panic bubbling through my body.

The moment I felt my chest tighten and that desperate need for air took control of my body, I lost what little calm I had left. I flailed about in the darkness, seeing nothing but my own demise closing in on me. That was, until I saw something flash in the corner of my eye.

A faint light glowed somewhere behind me, but each time I turned, I was greeted by more darkness. It took me a while to realize the glow came out of my backpack. I opened my bag, eyes widening at the sight of my notebook and pen pulsating softly with light. I opened my notebook and the light intensified so strongly, I couldn't keep my eyes open. The light drove the void away, and swallowed me whole.

CHAPTER 13

the Last Story
of a Promise

The first thing I did was suck in a deep breath of sweet, fresh air. I didn't care I nearly choked at the sudden influx of oxygen. My lungs burned and my body was sore, but I couldn't be happier to find myself in the middle of a fountain, water pouring over me from whimsical statues.

I was in the middle of a town square that looked very familiar. White buildings, decorated with multicolored gables and stained glass windows, surrounded me. The wreaths of light bulbs that hung from the crested roofs, and countless directional signposts betrayed the town's identity.

Though I was still panting and in shock over all of the events I had experienced, relief washed over me like a warm, relaxing shower.

"I'm back," I whispered, only now taking note of how people in the town square were staring at me, some in stunned amazement, others giggling. Some were even shaking their heads in disapproval.

Soaked to the bone, I got out of the fountain, trying to save whatever was left of my dignity. I checked my bag to make sure I had my notebook with me. I wasn't sure how I had gotten here, or why I was brought back to Wanderlost Borough, but I was so elated to see my notebook had survived the journey. Granted, there were only three stories scribbled down, but to imagine I had to visit three entirely new and enchanting worlds to collect them, made my skin break out in goosebumps.

When I flipped through the pages, none of the writing had been smudged. Either the notebook and pen I used were of an excellent waterproof quality, or this was nothing short of a small miracle made possible by magic.

I had just made the journey of a lifetime. As strange and as curious and confusing as it had been, I actually lived it. I got to listen to, and document, stories from worlds no one knew could possibly exist!

I paused when that realization sunk in, along with the last message given to me by that peculiar puppeteer.

The worlds you visited are dying. They thought your light could help fend off the darkness of oblivion that descended on these lands, but I see no greatness in you...

The light bulbs above me flickered again, as if merely remembering the words had an effect here, too.

"The worlds you visited are dying," I repeated softly, stroking the pages of my notebook. He wouldn't lie about something like that, would he?

Write. We'll be waiting.

He had been so reluctant to speak to me, so reluctant to tell me a story. He had tried to snub me the moment I had set foot in his caravan, and it took some convincing on my part to have him tell a story, after all.

Why would he suddenly want me to write, when the shadows were covering him from all sides like a massive claw?

I flipped through my notebook again, gasping when sparks of light flew from the pages where I had written the first story. The second story spewed out drops of water and tendrils of fire. The third, however, gave me the shivers, the music of an accordion playing softly from the pages. I closed the book quickly.

The Mythica had talked about the darkness that threatened the world, and the strangest man I had ever met had mentioned another Collector of Stories, one he deemed nasty and unwanted. It had been storming like crazy in the world of the cantankerous puppeteer, the darkness of the shadows so intense it felt like it could swallow up all that stood in its path.

If the puppeteer spoke the truth and all these worlds *were* at the brink of oblivion, then...Why did he tell *me* about it? Who was I to help out dying worlds? Why were they dying in the first place? Where did the darkness come from? What could I do to stop it?

Questions spun in my mind and a rush of anxiety overwhelmed me. I was a writer who had just been on an amazing adventure collecting stories. That's all I did. How could the responsibility of entire worlds suddenly rest on my shoulders?

Light flickered around me, and I jumped when a light bulb blew out. The sparks fell to the ground where I saw strange shadows shake and move away. There was so much more at play here, more than I had bargained for.

After all the things I experienced, why was I still apprehensive?

Heat seeped through my body when a newfound determination welled up from my chest. I closed the book with a clap and grabbed my backpack.

I had to travel back! Maybe there was a way to stop all of it, somehow. I looked around the old town of Wanderlost Borough, trying to retrace my steps so I could find the Way Fairgrounds again.

"Young writer, you've returned!" a voice called out. I was greeted by the sight of the merry Mayor of Wanderlost Borough, rushing to meet me. I didn't have the time to speak to him, however, not when there were more pressing matters that needed my attention.

"I have, and I'm afraid I have to leave again," I said.

The poor man was panting by the time he reached me, his face red. "Are you heading back home?" he asked through rasped breath, taking off his hat to wipe the sweat from his brow. There was something decidedly less cheerful about the mayor this time. Though he still smiled, his eyes stood worried as if he didn't want me to leave at all.

"No, I have to find a way to retrace the steps of my journey. I can't rightly explain but I fear the worlds I visited might be—"

"In danger?" he finished, the smile fading from his face as he sighed and nodded in understanding.

"You know about this?" I asked, my suspicion rising.

"Yes, I fear I do." He fiddled with his hat as he looked at me, scratching the back of his neck. "We were worried that perhaps you would not return from your journey. I told you it's been a long while since anyone came through our humble little town." He chuckled nervously, but there was fear and exhaustion in his eyes. His shoulders were sagging and his hands trembled. He took out a handkerchief to dab the sweat from his face.

"You never told me this town's story. Is there something I should know about?" I held onto my notebook, feeling an itch in my hand to get my pen.

The mayor sighed, clearly tired of keeping up a facade. He sat down on a stone bench, the streets around us all but silent. There were no people walking about anymore. Not even the wind dared make a sound.

"Wanderlost Borough, as I have told you, is a place specifically created for Wanderers like you. While this is certainly true, it is also a gateway to discover new worlds, connecting the universe together." He gazed up at me, before reaching out to grab my hand. "I know your journey must have been arduous, at best, but, would you mind listening to one last story, dear writer?"

His plea was so sincere, his face so sad, I felt compelled to comply. Though the other worlds may need the help, it seemed like Wanderlost Borough could use some aid as well. Maybe this place held the answers I was looking for.

"Follow me, I'd like to show you something," the mayor said.

He led the way through the still streets of Wanderlost Borough. Only now did I notice how the cobblestones gleamed in the twilight and the light bulbs, hanging from endless garlands. In a way, it seemed like the streets were paved in gold, while in truth, it must've just been raining, wet stones reflecting the light.

We arrived at the beautiful town hall and I tilted my head upon seeing the welcome sign. It hung a little crooked now and the gold lettering had faded.

How long had I been gone?

"Come, it's this way." The mayor spoke softly, opening the heavy door and urging me to enter. I blinked my eyes at the candles floating around the well-lit room. Each candle had a different colored flame dancing on its wick.

I had not expected to step into a grand library. Books reached all the way up the high ceiling, which congregated in a colorful dome of stained glass. My footsteps echoed through the great chamber on the shining marble floor, and when I looked down I could see my own, soaking wet reflection.

"How many books are there here?" I asked in awe. Bookshelves decorated the entire room and, upon closer inspection, I saw the bookshelves themselves were made out of books. I couldn't even see the walls of the building. I wondered if it even had walls.

"Oh, I would welcome you to count them if you had the patience and the time, but I fear we don't have that luxury right now." The mayor barked in a single chuckle, before he gestured toward a spiraling, brass staircase. "I do know that every story ever written by Wanderers passing our humble town is recorded here. The candlelight guards these books, so the darkness can never touch them."

Some candles flared up in brilliant sparks when shadows drew too near, true to the mayor's words. Darkness dispersed, unable to touch the countless books.

The staircase creaked under the mayor's weight, but it seemed stable enough to hold him. I was careful with my steps, as it was a long way down if we fell.

He led me through long corridors and narrow hallways, up more stairs than I cared to count, until we arrived at the bell tower. This chamber was a lot more modest than the library downstairs, but no less wondrous. The moment I stepped in, floating lights appeared out of nowhere, flowers smelling like honeysuckle grew near my feet and the scent of petrichor filled the air.

"What happened?" I asked as the images and scents faded again.

"This room is attuned to the memories and stories Wanderers have written. I believe it picked up on your adventures, my dear." The mayor waved his hand. "Come in, come in."

The mayor used the chamber as his office, that much was clear. There was a humble, oak desk placed in front of the window, from where one could see the entire town below. The view was breathtaking, and intriguing to see, as the countless roads that led out of the town interwove with one another, and yet ultimately seemed to lead to different destinations.

Behind the desk stood a magnificent, astrological clock that not only told the time, but showed the reigning constellations of the stars, each dot sparkling like lit up diamonds.

"Here." The mayor placed a warm towel over my shoulders and handed me a nice cup of tea. "Do take a seat."

"Thank you." I took a sip of the hot tea, smiling at the sight of a flower blooming inside the mug. I sat down and looked at the mayor, awkward moments passing between us before I found the courage to speak.

"You know, it just occurred to me I never asked for your name."

The mayor smiled again, nodding as he placed his hat on a stand by his desk. "It's quite all right. Most Wanderers come and go without ever learning it."

"Well, I'd like to know your name," I said, setting the tea down on the desk and extending my hand towards him. "My name is—"

"I know your name, and I am most honored you wish to learn mine." We shook hands as he bowed elegantly to introduce himself. "I am Horatio Helbram Faerbard, but do call me Horatio."

"Horatio," I repeated with a nod. "Very nice to meet you."

I took another sip of tea, wrapping myself up in the towel. "How is it that you know my name? Did you know I was coming, somehow?" I knew these were the questions I was supposed to ask when I first arrived in this enchanting place, but after coming back from the journey, the questions only now flooded in.

"I never know when a Wanderer enters our town," he said, "but I do always hope it."

There was that sad smile again.

Considering where he worked and how Wanderlost Borough looked, I wouldn't immediately assume there was anything wrong. Sure, some of the buildings and signs could use a little maintenance, but nothing that indicated any acute danger.

Then, the lights sputtered again.

The building shook, the bells trembling far above us.

"You said you wanted to tell me one last story." I cleared my throat, thinking of the warning of the puppeteer when I saw shadows flash by outside. "Is this a story I should be writing down?" I asked, though I wondered whether I had time for this.

"I don't believe it's necessary," Horatio said, looking at the clock before gazing back at me, "since you've lived this story yourself. But do write if that is your wish. My story will be brief. You see, before you arrived here, there was someone else that managed to find Wanderlost Borough. This was many years ago, I assume you would have still been a child."

I recalled a vague memory, but the image didn't come, like the word on the tip of your tongue that you just can't reach.

"There was something peculiar about this person. He was never meant to find the gateway, as he was no Wanderer." Horatio continued. I focused my attention back to him.

"He wasn't a Wanderer?"

"No, my dear, he was not. He might have been lost in many ways, but not the kind of lost you need to be if you wish to find this place. He came here, and did something bad," he trailed off into a whisper as though afraid the very person he spoke about might hear him.

"What did he do?" I whispered back.

Horatio leaned forward twirling his mustache in his fingers. "He was not a good man. He brought darkness with him wherever he went through the twisted stories he wrote, and with no one to counter his dark tales, no heroes to fight his villains, the shadows are free to fester in the worlds he visited." He scratched his chin. "For some reason, his true darkness thankfully spared Wanderlost Borough, though there are bits of his malice that lingered."

"Like those shadows I saw before, when I first came here. They were dancing."

"Exactly." Horatio nodded. "There used to be a time that Wanderlost Borough was filled with Wanderers like you, traveling to unknown worlds only each individual Wanderer could discover, but lately..." He sighed. "You are the first one to arrive, after that horrid man."

"Is he the Collector of Stories I heard about on my travels?" I tried to ignore the shiver that ran up my spine.

"If he is, I doubt it's only stories he collects. I believe he feeds off the misery, off the blackness in people's hearts. He's searching for something." Horatio groaned when he got out of his seat to walk toward a bookshelf, picking out a thick tome covered in dust.

Without even bothering to blow all the dust away, he simply opened it, flipping through the pages and returning to me.

"Some say he seeks for impossible things, a certain power he believes only storytellers—Wanderers—can give him," he said, pointing at a picture of a silhouette of a tall man, wearing a top hat which was very telling. He set the book in front of me and I studied it.

The pictures were painted in glimmering ink, giving something vibrant to the images, almost as if they were moving. While the silhouette of the man in the top hat was creepy, another figure caught my attention. Someone hooded in a cloak made of shadows, decorated with gems of light. Nostalgia hit me, but I couldn't place it.

Who would have thought that my collection of stories would end with something so grave?

"Stories that Wanderers gathered are never released out into the world because of him, and without readers—Wayfarers—to read the stories that the Wanderers so arduously collected, the light of the world fades, granting the darkness more power. I fear that it now might grant *him* more power as well." Horatio's voice was full of concern. He looked at me a moment and grabbed my hand. "That's why it was such a relief to see you reappear in our town again." He took the book from me so he could store it.

"Why hasn't anyone tried to stop him?" I asked, unable to shake the feeling of trepidation and dread now.

"Someone has definitely tried. It is said that this entity of darkness is now trapped within a story. But to defeat him, light must be brought to the worlds he's visited, to the worlds he's tainted, otherwise—"

As if on cue, the lights flickered again, longer this time, more erratically. Outside, I heard something falling. Glancing out the window, some of the directional boards had fallen from the buildings.

I turned to a worried Horatio Helbram Faerbard, feeling anxious myself. "What will happen if this world and others cease to exist?"

There was a heartbroken smile on his face, unshed tears forming in his eyes. All he could do was shake his head, no words able to come out of his mouth.

"What can I do to help?" I asked, though the cowardly part of me wanted to ask a different question altogether. Perhaps it was because I didn't want the worlds I'd seen to perish before I had a chance to tell others about them, or perhaps it was because, in my arrogance, I thought I could actually do something to help them. It would be nice to prove that puppeteer wrong.

Seeing Horatio's face, so fragile and deeply sorrowful, my sense of sympathy won out over the part that just wanted to run back home.

"Drink your tea, my dear," was his unconventional answer.

"Huh?" I inquired oh-so intelligently.

"Drink." He pushed the tea toward me and I did as I was told. The tea was soothing and warmed me up, though I did wait for something to happen, just in case. When nothing did, I set down the cup and frowned at him.

"Was that it?"

He shook his head. "Now, you write." He opened my notebook and flipped through all the pages. "Do not let the magic between these sheets of paper escape. The stories you collected are merely the tip of an iceberg. There are other stories of these worlds that you need to tell, and once you do, Wayfarers will come. They will take the road you traveled first, share the journey, and maybe some of them will become Wanderers themselves, going on their own adventures to collect their own stories."

"I don't think I understand. Shouldn't I go back to the worlds I visited before and see how I can help them?"

"You will travel to them, have no fear." His voice was warm and calm, but I was still confused.

"Then, I should get going, shouldn't I?"

I felt the sweat breaking out like a cold sheen of ice when Horatio shook his head. "While your journey is not over, you are not the hero these worlds need. They need to find their own light to battle the darkness threatening their worlds. I believe you are tasked to help find these new heroes and to write their stories. Battle the stories of the darkness with stories of the light." He leaned forward.

I glanced at the pages of the notebook, each story carefully documented. I might have written them down, but they had their own heroes. It was Keiana who defeated Nepherox, it were Te'Kala and Letheon who overcame Te'Irena's madness, and in the last one, it was Raku whose love for writing became his downfall.

Was this truly how I could help? By writing new stories to counter the ones he came up with?

Biting my lip, I glanced at Horatio, doubt pressing against my chest. "Why me? I mean, I do want to help, but am I the right person for this? Can I truly help?"

Horatio chuckled softly, a gentle look in his eyes. "You are the first to come here after such a long time, and you managed to return here after your journey. You saw the light in the stories you collected, you refused to be intimidated by the darkness that trailed it. If not you, my dear, then I don't know who."

A blush crept up my cheeks. I think he gave me too much credit there. "I only wrote down what others told me..."

"Any story told can be interpreted in many ways. It all depends on which version you were most drawn to."

I pursed my lips together, absently fidgeting with my shirt. Assuming what the mayor said was true, I might not have been able to come back here, if I had focused more on the dark elements of the stories.

I shuddered. "And what about finding my way home?"

At this, Horatio put the pen in my hand and smiled. "Write, Wanderer, and you'll always find your way home."

The bells tolled softly in the tower, their vibrations shaking within my chest. I watched how Wanderlost Borough sunk into the darkness of the night, the light bulbs doing their utmost to shine as brightly as they could.

I watched the beautiful landscape come to life, stared out into the horizon of the trees and mountains, of the lakes that lay sprawled amidst the forests, but in my mind I was already traveling back to the worlds I visited. I found their names in the clouds, in the ashes of a burning fire, in the roots of trees hidden deep below the ground.

I wasn't sure before, but I had found the stories that lay waiting for me to write them, the stories that now burned inside me and needed to be told.

"Write them," Horatio said as if he could tell those stories were seeping into my mind. "Write them and send the light to us, like you're already doing." He smiled encouragingly, though I was too confused and dazed to ask what he meant.

"Take the Wayfarers on your journey with you, those who scan their curious eyes over these words, driven by a spirit of adventure, guided by a lust for more than their current world has to offer them." The tolling of the bells started to drown out his imploring voice.

"And write, Wanderer. Always keep writing…"

I vaguely nodded, grabbing my pen with the intention to write, but, try as I might, I couldn't keep my eyes open. The world started to spin around me, Horatio's voice urging me to write echoing in time with the loud tolling of the bells.

When I grasped my pen and attempted to put it to paper, I accidentally knocked over the tea, the purple flower falling out of it. I remembered its scent, though I didn't know why I did. Sounds around me grew heavier, images became blurred, though I saw Horatio's mustache, his warm smile, his kind eyes, and his soft mumbling plea to write.

The world fell away from me, and clutching my notebook and pen, I fell with it.

Epilogue

Would you have expected this story to end the way it did? Neither did I.

I started my journey in search for new worlds and more stories to tell. I had looked for the portal from my childhood, letting my faith and belief guide the way. Looking back now, I achieved exactly what I wanted. I did see new, magical, and mysterious worlds. I did collect more stories and write them all down in my notebook. But my journey didn't lead me to the happy, fulfilled ending I had hoped for. Instead, the path I treaded opened up more roads to follow, little more than a scratch on the surface of more intricate worlds and stories.

Did your spark reach those worlds, I wonder? Did the stories set your imagination on fire, Wayfarer?

Fire is dangerous, you know, but I suppose, so is the water. It was water that brought me to Wanderlost Borough, and it was water that sent me back...

I couldn't tell you what had happened to me after I lost consciousness and woke up in a crystal clear lake, as still as a glass mirror. I floated in the middle of it, waking up to the sight of thick leaves, so densely grown the rays of the sun could barely shine through them. I saw a flash of a grinning frog, being carried away by a beautiful blue bird, but when I startled into full consciousness, I was entirely alone.

I didn't rightly know whether I was still somewhere in Wanderlost Borough, or had traveled to another world, until the solitude brought me to my senses—well, what was left of them, anyway.

Should I tell you that I wrote the stories that burned in my mind, that took control over my hand, my fingers, as if I were a puppet on a string?

Should I tell you that, even now, I still need your curiosity, your sense of adventure, and your endless love of stories to guide not just your way, but mine and that of unsung heroes yet to come, as well?

After having experienced a most wondrous, absolutely curious adventure, at the end of it all, it feels like I ended where I began: a little lost, but determined to write more. Just like Horatio said, battle the stories of darkness, with the stories of light. It might take time until that darkness is defeated, but I suppose I'll have to tackle it one world at a time.

After all, I've learned that if darkness is closing in, it must be countered by light. If fire burns, let it at least be the all-consuming blaze of love, for it creates more than it destroys. Death is a friend, but be wary of those mysterious men who wear top hats and give one the promise of immortality.

Given, the last lesson is a strange one to have learned, but a good one, just in case.

Do I still have your attention, Wayfarer? Or did I lose you to the madness?

Persevere, Wayfarer, for my job as a writer is not nearly as complicated and crucial as yours will be.

Adventure will always wait at the turning of the page. Danger will always lurk within the blackness of the ink, and while I don't know where my next endeavor will take me, I do know my journey hasn't ended yet.

Worlds are stretched out in my mind's eye, fighting against oblivion, waiting to be discovered by other Wayfarers, waiting to be reborn again.

A storm is raging as I write these words, the thunder rolling and the lightning flashing amidst the endless darkness, but I do not fear it as I used to.

I put my pen to paper, writing the first words to find those brave souls to join the universes hidden in these pages.

I still hope that you'll be the one to join me...

How curious of you, Wayfarer,
to have chosen my chronicles to add to your collection...

Now, are you ready to collect some more?

Discover the Worlds

Look for more stories to collect from our
Wandering author in the future.
The heroes have been found.
Their stories are waiting to be told.

Each journey starts with the first step.
Don't be afraid to take it.

www.wanderlostborough.com

Acknowledgements

My love for stories began long before I even knew how to write and I have my parents to thank for that. With a solid upbringing of one bedtime story per night (thanks, Mom!) and lots of TV-shows and Disney movies after school (thanks, Dad!), my love for the art of storytelling flourished.

I'm sure they've had many sleepless nights and constant worries floating in their heads when I announced, after graduating from Uni with an MSc degree in Neuropsychology, that I was going to be a fulltime writer. Instead of trying to talk me out of it, I've received nothing but unconditional love and tireless support. There's not enough words in this universe to express my gratitude so for now, this will have to do:

Mom, Dad, I did it~! Thank you for your patience, support and trust in me. I'll always strive to do better, to never give up, and keep chasing my dreams because I know they can become real— a lesson I've learned, thanks to you.

The path of a writer is an arduous one, and at times it can be quite lonely. I am sappy enough to boldly state that I really wouldn't know what to do without my tribe of sisters from other misters. I'm truly blessed to have these ladies in my life— we're gonna grow old together, might as well get used to it. Warning: Beware the cheese in 3, 2, 1...!

To my Alpha Beta Reader Supreme Izzy, even if I've thanked you countless times already, allow me to do so again because I want you to be disgustingly honored and you rightly deserve to be called out on how awesome you are. You've read every letter, brainfart, panic attack, and word vomit with the patience and meticulousness of a true goddess. Thank you for often figurately smacking some sense into me, for your contagious enthusiasm, and endless support. Dragons rule, and so do you!

Thank you, my metal-loving, rocking-at-life and musically gifted sisje, for having faith in me, for your active support, for the brainstorm sessions, and for always being upfront and honest to me about my work. Our late-night conversations were food for the soul (and tummies, because food—OMG so much yummy food...), and your genuine interest and enthusiasm invigorated me to keep on trucking. Thank you for having my back!

No matter how tired I became, frustrated, or doubted my work and skills as a writer, I could always count on my chubba cosmic twin to be there for me with a delicious homemade cup of coffee, an understanding, listening ear, and advice to spare. Your unconditional encouragements mean the world and more. Thank you for always taking the time, for always opening your door, and for always looking out for me— you are my person.

I'd also like to thank my sweet, big sister who generously gifted me the book cover almost immediately when she heard I was serious about becoming a writer. Your generosity and kindness are a true inspiration.

I wish I could dedicate pages filled with my sincere gratitude to those amazingly wonderful readers who helped me shape, polish, and scrutinize the manuscript to be able to confidently present it in its current form. Thank you to all my beta readers for your valuable feedback and for enduring my overly extensive, borderline obsessive, supercalifragilisticexpialidociously frequent use of dialogue tags and adverbs. Your insights have been worth their weight in gold, thank you so much for being awesome.

Thank you, Kat, for your patience, your guiding hand, and for tirelessly editing my book.

To my fantastic and talented CPs: R.J. Ford, who scoured through the manuscript with the eyes of a hawk, gave me brutal honesty when needed and uplifting comments of encouragement: *hannon le, mellon nîn.* EL Rowe, whose insights, suggestions and constructive criticisms really helped in fine-tuning the story—thank you. Jackie Ito, thank you for your hard work, suggestions and lovely comments. I feel so lucky to have met you all!

And last, but certainly never least, thank *you* for picking up this book and giving it a chance. Thank you for allowing me to share pieces of my world with you, and I hope you've enjoyed going on this fantastical journey with our elusive writer. There are a lot more adventures (and *dragons*) waiting on the horizon, and I certainly hope you'll join me again for the ride.

About the Author

Gabriella Michaelis is an up and coming fantasy author who is devoted to take readers on imaginative, curious adventures within fantastical realms where danger always lurks and heroes are found in unexpected ways. Her stories are guaranteed fantasy — just a little more peculiar, with perhaps, a sprinkle of spooky.

Chronically suffering from wanderlust, she draws her inspiration from her travels, while exploring the extraordinary in the ordinary. This, combined with her love for '80s fantasy movies, gave birth to her first book-baby, *The Curious Chronicles of Curious Tales*.

When not having late-night discussions with her headstrong characters or plotting the next books to fling them into, Gabriella is a self-proclaimed fun-loving nerd who adores movies, games, music, and traveling, with theme parks being one of her most favorite destinations. She loves to connect with her readers, especially if they're as crazy about dragons as she is.

Visit her website and get in touch through social media!

www.wanderlostborough.com

Instagram: @Myth.Hikari
Twitter: @Myth_Hikari